THE CO

 GW00871150

A NOTE ON THE AUTHOR

Eilís Dillon was born in Galway. She is one of Ireland's leading writers, having published many children's and adult novels, as well as poetry, plays and short stories. She recently won the Irish Children's Book Trust Bisto Book of the Year Award.

THE CORIANDER

EILÍS DILLON

Children's
POOLBEG

First published 1963
by Faber and Faber Limited, London

This edition 1992 by
Poolbeg Press Ltd, Knocksedan House
Forrest Great, Swords, Co Dublin

ISBN 1 85371 214 0

A Catalogue record for this book is available from the British Library

Poolbeg Press receives financial assistance from
The Arts Council/An Chomhairle Ealaíon, Dublin

Cover design by Carol Betera
Typeset by Mac Book Limited in ITC Stone 10/14
Printed by the The Guernsey Press Company Ltd
Vale, Guernsey, Channel Islands

Chapter One

No one on our island will ever forget the wreck of the *Coriander*. It's not that we are unaccustomed to wrecks. We get plenty of them, not only because we are the most westerly island off the Galway coast but also because some special currents and winds send the unfortunate ships straight for our rocky shores, when the winter gales are howling. The Captains know us, however, and they make sure to keep out of our way. So the men of our island say who have sailed in ships. Big John Moran who rose to be second mate in an English grain ship, and enjoys a fine pension ever since he retired—Big John said that his Captains always used to say:

"There's the Killaney Light. There's one light I never like to see too plain."

This meant that they were in too close, and they would make off out to sea again as fast as they could.

Killaney is the outermost tip of Inishgillan. We all know that Killaney means "the cell of Enda," that is our own Saint Enda, and no relation of the Aran Island Enda.

No one at all seems to know what Inishgillan means. Inish is the Irish word for an island but whether there was a saint called Gillan, or whether the shape of the island

accounts for its name, has never been decided. Some of
the scholars are arguing and fighting about it to this day,
so I've been told. One lot are on the side of Saint Gillan,
but no one can prove that such a person ever lived. The
other lot say that Inishgillan means the island shaped
like a cut seed-potato, which is "sciollán" in Irish.

I have always been more inclined to believe these last
ones. The cut side of the potato you might say is the sheer
cliff that faces the Atlantic, and that breaks the force of
the wind so that our houses are not all tumbled off into
the sea. From the cliff, the island slopes gently downwards,
and there is a sort of wide cleft where the road runs up.
Most of the houses are on either side of this road. We
have no pier but on the leeward side of the island there
is a long slip. Beside it there is a sandy beach, and this is
where we keep our currachs. No one on Inishgillan has
a hooker, nor any kind of sailing boat. If anyone were to
build a hooker, that man would be wasting his time and
money. The first September storm would knock it to
pieces, and every man on the island would be picking up
the wreck for a week. In Clare Island they can have
sailing boats, and in Inishbofin too. Those places have
little sheltered harbours. The biggest Aran Island has a
pier so that the steamer can come right in and tie up to
it. The people of that island are fine and wealthy, with
boats of all descriptions, and slated houses, but we don't
envy them. We find that having no pier keeps the
visitors away, and that is how we like it.

Still, for a long time before the *Coriander* was wrecked,
we had been discussing the drawbacks to our remoteness
from the mainland, and one drawback in particular was
that no doctor could be persuaded to come and live on
Inishgillan. We had no teacher either, at the time of the

wreck, but we were never without one for more than a few months and no one grudged the children their holidays from school. We knew that a teacher would appear without warning one day and imprison them all again. The question of the doctor was different. The Government had promised us a doctor. We all saw the advertisement in the *Connacht Tribune*, which was brought to us by Willie O'Connell in the lifeboat along with the post. But no doctor arrived.

"Who'd come out here?" Willie said. "'Tis too far from any place."

"'Tis near enough to my house," said Big John Moran. "There's many a good man was born and reared here."

"Now, there you have something," said Willie. "If a man was born and reared here, he wouldn't mind living here, but for a man that would be used to the city, 'twould drive him out of his mind. No sound all day but the howling of the wind and the waves and the seagulls."

"And the yapping of Willie O'Connell the day the lifeboat would be in," said Big John. "How do the rest of us live, I'd like to know? I've lived in New York and London and Shanghai, and I never met a righter, tighter place to spend my days than Inishgillan."

"Tight is right," said Willie. "Did ye pay the rates yet?"

"No doctor, no rates," said Big John. "That was the decision and we're sticking to it."

"Ye'll save a mint of money. The Lord spare ye from ever getting a doctor!"

Willie lived on Inishmore, which is the biggest Aran Island. As well as having the pier, they have a motor-car there, and three Civic Guards, which makes them feel superior.

Still, Big John was never angry with Willie. He always

came down to the slip when he saw the lifeboat plunging along towards the slip, and they enjoyed sparring with each other about anything and everything.

Luke Hernon, the postmaster, was there that same day, collecting the mailbag from Willie. Luke never argued. Because of being a Civil Servant, he had a feeling that he must be equally friendly with everyone. He lived in the next house to ours and I always came down to the slip with him to collect the bags.

This time there were three of them, well-laden, though Christmas was over a fortnight ago. I loved the heavy bags that came after Christmas, because there was always a chance that one of my uncles in Portland, Maine, might have forgotten some special thing that he had spotted in a shop, after he had sent his main parcel. Once or twice this did happen, but usually the bags were full of parcels and letters that had been delayed by bad weather, or else they were from people who were noted for their lateness in everything.

It was the same story this time. When I went around the island with Luke, that same afternoon, the women came running to the doors to receive their parcels. Old Mamó said:

"Wisha, Tomeen will be late for his own funeral."

"But he'll be there, all right," said Luke, "and that's the main thing."

"'Tis, sure," said Mamó. "'Tis, I suppose. But 'twas a fright to be trying to make all the children come in time to school, and my own son to be always leggety-last. Ten o'clock he'd come loping in, after I seeing him leave home before myself at half past eight. It was thirty years before he told me where he used to be those mornings, and even then he wrote it in a letter from the New World, for fear of what I'd do to him."

"Where used he be, Mamó?" I asked, for I had never heard this story.

"Down the cliffs, sucking seagulls' eggs, if 'twas the right time of the year, and—oh, I'm ashamed to say it!"

She threw her apron over her face to cover the blushes. Mamó is the name of all our grandmothers but she was a special kind, for she had taught the infants in the school for sixty years, since she was a young girl with a plait down her back. Tomeen was her only son.

"Go on, Mamó," said Luke. "Isn't he the pride of the Boston police now? We won't write and tell them what he used to be doing when he was a young fellow."

Luke winked at me, so that I guessed he knew what the crime was. Mamó took down the apron and said shyly:

"Going around the nests of my own neighbours' hens, sucking the eggs in the early morning. That's how he grew so fine and big and strong. And I used to be so proud of him, thinking it was the potatoes and fish and buttermilk and stirabout were doing it for him."

"I suppose they were doing a share of it," said Luke.

The mention of food reminded her to invite us in for a cup of tea. Luke had left her parcel till the last, knowing that this would happen, and there would be no question of refusing the invitation. The only way to make sure that the other households would not be kept waiting for their letters and parcels was to go to them first.

Mamó fussed around us happily.

"Into the hob with you, Lukeen. Pull over the little stool, Patcheen, while I fatten up the fire a bit."

Mamó called everyone by their baby-names, which were the names by which she had known them first. There was some excuse for doing this with me because though I was sixteen years old at that time, I had still a few inches to grow. Besides, to her way of thinking it probably seemed that only yesterday I had been sitting in a skirt on one of the little benches in her part of the school. To me it seemed like an age, and it must have seemed a lifetime to Luke, who was a man of forty-five.

Mamó had retired only four years before this, and I think she missed the bustle of school and the company of the children. She built up a big fire and hung the kettle on the crane above it. Then she settled down on the other hob to chat with us.

"Tell me now, what news had Willie for you?"

"Three English trawlers and five Spanish ones are sitting inside at Kilronan this minute, he says, and hardly a stir out of the sea. The fish are running well, but they won't go out."

"Lazy they are, I suppose, after the Christmas," said Mamó, drawing on her experience at school.

"'Tisn't that at all," said Luke, "but a big storm they say is coming in from the Atlantic."

"Thanks be to God they're in out of it. 'Tis a terrible thing to say, but I'd love the storms only for thinking of the poor sailors. I'd love to be lying there in bed, listening to the wind, knowing the thatch is good. The roar of the wind makes me feel I could fly away with it, over to Russia, maybe, or up to the North Pole where they have all the snow. Isn't that queer talk for an old woman?"

I was very glad to hear this, for I secretly loved storms myself, and I had long been afraid that some day soon I would get sense, and would never enjoy them again.

"What other news had he? Was he over in Bofin?" Mamó was asking.

"He was, faith, but sure nothing ever happens in Bofin."

"Not a wedding? Not a wake or a funeral?"

"A wedding there was, between Bartley Conneeley Pat and Winnie MacDonagh."

"You mean old Winnie, that's home from America five years?"

"Yes, indeed. Herself and Bartley are married at last, but 'twas so long expected there was hardly anyone took any notice when it came about."

"Ay, they're slow in Bofin," said Mamó. "Did Willie know about our sheep?"

"Faith, then, if he did he said nothing to me," said Luke. "And I didn't tell him a word about it."

Suddenly the two of them rounded on me.

"Did you tell him about the sheep, Pat?"

"Not a word," I said indignantly. "Didn't I know that no word was to be said about them? And anyway, weren't you right there by my side, every minute that Willie was at the ship?"

"I was, indeed," said Luke.

"Don't be cross, agrá," said Mamó. "It's only that we don't want the Bofin people, and the Aran people to be laughing at us."

Just then the kettle boiled. She jumped up and got the teapot, and cut soda-bread for all of us, and buttered it with her own salty butter which was famous all over Connacht. It seemed to me that she gave me extra rations, either to prove that she trusted me, or else to ensure my continued silence.

The question of the sheep was a sore one with us. It had spoiled every bit of fun on Inishgillan for the last nine months, because no one had the heart to get up a dance or a party while it remained unsolved. All through the long summer, when we should have been having music and dancing down on the flags by the sea, or in someone's kitchen, there was nothing but little groups of men leaning against the walls in the evenings, and all talking about the same thing.

A mile and a half away, to the south-east of Inishgillan, there is an island that belongs by long, long tradition to us. It is about three miles long and a mile and a half wide, which is the same size as the middle Aran Island. There is short, sweet grass there, fine for sheep. This is very valuable grass to us, because we have little enough of it on Inishgillan. When the lambs reach a reasonable size, about March or April, we lay straw mats in the currachs to save them from their sharp little feet, and then we bring them and the ewes over to the Grazing Island for the rest of the summer. There is no other name on that island but the Grazing Island, which I think proves that no one ever lived there. If they had, it would surely be called after a saint. Every man on our island has a right to bring his sheep there. This had been happening in the memory of all our great-great-grandfathers and never a sheep had been lost. But now, since last year, they had begun to disappear.

After the first lot went, the men thought it was down over the cliff they had gone. A search was made, but nothing was found, and the tide brought in no carcasses. More went a few weeks later, and then more again. No one had been able to discover what had been happening to them, and the mystery was giving everyone the creeps. Mothers were bringing their children in long before dark, as if they were afraid that the fairies would take them. The men whose sheep had disappeared were beginning to look with suspicion on their more fortunate neighbours. Hard words had been said more than once and it almost seemed that out island was on the brink of civil war.

As usual, mention of the lost sheep put an end to our conversation with Mamó. After a silence, Luke stood up. We thanked her for the tea, and went outside. Only when we were gone would politeness allow her to open her parcel.

Mamó's house was at the top of the road, the highest house on the island. She was well sheltered by the hills on either side of her, but still, when we stepped outside that evening, the wind was already whistling through the bare branches of her little apple tree, and whirling around the corner of the house so that the hens and ducks had gone into the cart shed for shelter. Luke leaned in over the half-door again and said:

"There's a storm coming, right enough. Would you like to come down to our place for the night?"

"Not at all," said Mamó, "I'll lock the two doors and I'll be fine."

As we walked down the hill, the Killaney light was flashing against a lead-coloured sea, pitted and patched with white foam. The lighthouse stood on a little platform of rock, and a tall column of spray shot into the air with every big wave that struck the rock. Long practice had taught us that you could measure the violence of the sea by the height of the column of spray. This evening it reached almost to the top of the lighthouse. Then it fell, in a slow, beautiful fan-shaped scatter of drops, lit up to silver by the last of the cold sunlight.

"'Tis a wicked sea," said Luke. "Thank God the trawlers had warning of it." He stopped suddenly, and stood with a finger pointing. "Look! Look! There's a ship!"

"A trawler?"

"That's no trawler! She'd make ten of any of the Spanish trawlers. God save us! What is she doing?"

"Making for Galway, maybe."

"Faith and if she is, she's on the wrong tack. Over by Aran she should be."

We watched her for a while as she came on. She was three-quarters of a mile away when we saw her first, and every minute showed her coming closer. There was nothing we could do. You can't stand half-way along an island like ours, and shout instructions to a foolish sea captain.

"The lightkeepers will see her. They should radio to her to keep off. Oh, keep off! Keep off!"

Luke hardly knew what he was doing. He began to run down the road, shouting as he went, so that the people came running to their doors. They all looked out to sea at once, seeing where Luke was pointing, and then they followed him down the hill, all the way down to the slip.

There Luke stopped. By this time, waves ten feet high were galloping in onto the strand, splashing and roaring and whirling so that the look of them would frighten the heart in you. They ran shining up the concrete slip, and then the water poured in sheets of foam over the sides of it, and went roaring back into the sea with the waves on the strand.

"She's coming straight for the Three Rocks," said Luke, and his voice was nearly gone from him now.

"We'd best telegraph for the Aran lifeboat," said Bartley MacDonagh. "Let you go back up this minute, Luke, and do that."

"I should have stopped to do it on the way down," said Luke. "'Twould have been more sensible than running here like a madman. Bartley, let you go round to the Three Rocks—or better, wait here for a few minutes. Maybe with God's help she'll round them safely. If you think she won't make it, go around there and be ready to give help—"

"We'll do what's right, Luke," said Bartley quietly. "Off with you now."

Luke went off, and the men huddled together, watching. The women stood in a group apart from the men. There were several boys there who were big enough to be useful. I went over to join these. We were very frightened. We had often picked up pieces of timber, ropes and all sorts of bits of cargo, washed up on the strand, and surely a proof that some ship had been wrecked within recent weeks. We always carried these home in great triumph. We hardly thought where they had come from, but we did know that they added a few necessary things to our way of living. Every timber water-bucket, every oar, and a good many of the rafters of our houses had come sailing in to us in this way. But it was a different thing to see a fine hearty ship, with the bloom of health on her, go crashing to pieces right before our eyes.

That was exactly what we saw. Soon the ship was so near that we could see several people gathered by the rail. Lights were on all over her, showing from every porthole. I went over to Luke's nephew, Roddy, who was my great friend. We were the same age, and we had been in the same class at school together.

"Why doesn't she turn out to sea?" I shouted above the horrid noise of the wind.

"Maybe the wind is too strong, or maybe her propeller is broken. She seems very helpless. She's foundering like a harpooned shark."

"They're lowering the boats!" one of the men shouted.

"We needn't watch that," I said, and I began to run along the strand towards the Three Rocks.

The thought of watching the boats trying to cross that patch of snarling sea made me feel a little queer in the head. No one on shore would be able to do anything but wait, and wonder whether the boats would ever rise up out of the sea again, after each time that they disappeared in the hollow of the waves. Then when they capsized, as they surely would, they would have to watch the people struggling in the water, and not be able to move a finger to help them. It seemed to me that that was women's work.

"Come on," I called out over my shoulder. "We might be some way useful when she strikes."

By this time there was no doubt that she would strike. Beyond the Three Rocks there was a clear hundred yards of huge, tumbled boulders, half-covered now by the rising tide. The Three Rocks were fifty yards out from the shore. They were set in a triangle, the smallest one in front, twenty feet high, and the two bigger ones a little behind. The sea swirled in and out between them, always following the same pattern, where the current moved. Even on a reasonably calm day, a man in a currach would not dare to go close to the Three Rocks, because after a certain point, he would be sucked along with the current. Wrack came in there very often.

We joined the group of men standing on the short grass above the shore. Not one of them would look at the man beside him for fear of seeing the terrible excitement in his eyes. The same thought was running through all their minds:

"God save all the decent men on this ship from

drowning, but Lord of Heaven! What a prize you're sending us!"

My own father was there and he drew me in to stand beside him. When the first crash came, I found myself gripping his hand as I had not done since I was a small boy.

It was a terrible sound, the rending and smashing of the metal plates. The ship seemed to start back, as a man might if he stepped on a snake. Then she came forward again with another crash, and another, as if she was determined to knock off her own nose against the outer rock.

It was no more than five o'clock, but the daylight was nearly gone. The thought crossed my mind that if the people from the ship were not ashore before dark, there would be no hope for them.

Suddenly all the lights in the ship went out. Still she went on battering herself on the outer rock. The men who had been at the rail had gone. I dared not turn my head to see whether they had reached the strand. Not a sign of life showed on the ship.

"I wonder did they all leave her?" John Connor said. "I wonder is there anyone on her at all?"

Then an extraordinary thing happened. The ship withdrew from the shore, sucked back by some freak wave or other. She must have been badly holed by the bows, for she was carrying her stern high and we could see her decks sloping downwards towards us. Then, in one long awful sweep, she made straight for the shore to the right of the Three Rocks. She never stopped until she hit the boulders, and after that she did not move again, but stuck there, wedged so tightly that even that wicked sea could not get another stir out of her.

No one had hoped for this. Indeed it put us in a difficulty because there was a danger that she could be salvaged. The men began to mutter among themselves. So long as there was a possibility of salvage, there could be no hope of acquiring her as wrack.

"Such a storm I never saw," said Sidecar. "You'd think it would be able to break up a bit of a ship like that."

Sidecar was not very sensible at the best of times. He had another name, but he was always known as Sidecar because of his wish, so often expressed, for a sidecar to drive in, in the evenings. The fact that we had only one road did not lessen his longing for it. Now everyone clearly wished he had not spoken. Wrack had to come from God, and they felt that there was something wrong in expressing a wish for it.

"I'm thinking she'll hold there for a while," said Big John after a moment. "We'd best go back to the slip and find out what happened to the unfortunate people who took to the boats."

There had been two boats, and the first news we heard at the slip was that one of them had actually reached the strand. How it happened, no one knew. It was just handed along from one wave to the next, and then it came riding in to the shore with the white-faced men clinging to the thwarts, not able to lift a finger to help themselves. Only at the very edge of the sea, the boat overturned, and the men were rolled out into the water. They were soaked through, walking up and down and stamping their feet, and swearing that they would never go to sea again.

The ship was from South America, with a mixed cargo for Bristol. The sailors were all nationalities, several Americans and English, and an Indian, who was a great curiosity for us who had never seen the like before, and an Irishman from Tory Island, off the coast of Donegal. Luke was back at the slip by this time, and was trying to console the men at the loss of their ship and of their comrades in the second boat.

"Isn't it a great thing for ye to be alive?" he said. "Everyone's time will come to die, and it was their time, and that's all that can be done about it. Let ye all come up to my house now, and drink tea and get warm by the fire, and we'll find a shakedown for the night for every one of ye. The lifeboat will come for ye in the morning and take ye into Galway. That's a fine city, and there's every kind of people there to help ye. Some of us will stay here and watch in case anyone is washed in from the other boat. Come along now, come along."

And so he got them to leave the slip and go in a little depressed group up the hill to his cottage.

Big John and Bartley stayed by the slip, with one or two others. All of the women went with the rest, up the hill. They were moaning a little among themselves at the loss of the second boat, and the sound made me feel so sad that I could not bear to go with them, though I would have liked to hear the men talk. There would be good talk later on, when the good drop from the bottle would be mixed with their tea, and they would begin to tell about the wreck.

In the last of the daylight, I turned aside and went to have another look at the ship where she was wedged between the rocks. In a moment I noticed that Roddy Hernon was following me, and I waited for him.

"I can't stand the old ones' ologoning," I said.

"I felt a bit like ologoning myself," said Roddy. "'Tis a terrible thing the way the second boat was there one minute and was gone the next. I heard them saying 'twas like a huge hand would pull it down into the sea."

This was such a horrid thought that it put every other one out of my mind. We climbed the little shoulder of ground that was between the strand and the rocky shore beyond. Now we kept closer down by the rocks, to get a better view of the ship. We stared at her in the gloom, trying to read her name, but we could not make it out. This was why we were almost upon the man before we saw him.

He was crawling like a crab among the great black boulders. But for the storm he would have been above the high-water mark, but with that heavy sea and with the thundering wind, the waves were running almost up to the grass, in and out between the boulders. One moment he was high and dry, and the next moment the sea was flowing over him, knocking him flat, rolling him along, battering him nearly senseless. Each time this happened he heaved himself up on his elbows and crawled another piece, more slowly, until the sea came up again.

We said no word to each other, but went bounding down to him, skipping from rock to rock when we could, wading waist-high in water when we had to go between the rocks. Saving our breath, we seized him under the arms, and began to drag him towards the shore. He gave a single, terrible cry of pain, and then he must have fainted, for we heard no more from him while we got him up onto the grass, out of reach of that wicked, cruel sea.

Though he was a thin man, it had given us all we could do to beach him. We were panting for breath, but there was no time to waste. We turned him over and began to press his ribs to get the water out of him and to get the air into him. We were experts at this, because Big John had shown us how to do it. The man revived after a while, and looked quickly from one of us to the other. There was no moment of wondering where he was or what had happened. He had a thin, sharp face, like a seagull, and bright brown eyes. Some kind of a scar by the side of his mouth gave him an ugly, twisted look but we soon saw that this was an accidental expression and had nothing to do with his state of mind.

"Thanks," he said, in a gasping half-whisper. "I saw you coming. I thought you wouldn't get to me in time." He coughed. "I'm full of sea-water. That doesn't matter. It's my leg is the trouble. The shin-bone is broken."

"Maybe it's only bruised," said Roddy.

"No, it's broken all right. I know it is. Now we won't argue about it. Just take me to a house and I'll tell you what to do about it. Is there a doctor anywhere near?"

"There's one on Bofin Island, but he can't come till the sea goes down."

"Well, we'll have to manage without. I'll tell you exactly what to do, and you'll do it without argument. I can't bear argument. Well, what are you waiting for? Get under my arms, one at each side." He looked at us more kindly and said: "Don't be afraid. I'm a doctor myself, and I'll tell you exactly what to do. I have one good leg, and I'll help you by hopping on that. Come along, now!"

"We'll take him to Mamó's house," I said, without looking at Roddy.

In that moment, he understood what was in my mind. He answered without looking at me:

"Yes, that will be a good place to take him."

Without another word, we leaned down and took the

doctor under the arms again, and somehow got him upright. Then, half-carrying him, we set out along the path by the shore, away from the slip.

Chapter Two

Mamó's house was the farthest house from the slip, as I have said, and the highest house on the island. Many times on the way there, the unfortunate doctor asked piteously:

"Are we coming to the house? Is it much farther?"

Each time we had to let him lie on the ground for a few minutes, to collect strength to go on again. The path led along the top of the shore for a quarter of a mile, and then it began to mount parallel to the road but well below it. The lights of the houses that bordered the road were not visible from the path, even if the doctor had known in which direction to look for them. The black flank of the island rose steeply on our left, and the sea raved and spat below us on our right. It was pitch dark, except when the Killaney light swung sharply across and lit up the island and the white-painted sea for a few seconds. This light was enough to show us our way.

Now when I look back on it, it seems to me that we were quite heartless in what we did that evening. We were so much carried away by the idea that had taken hold of us, that we could think of nothing else. Our island had always needed a doctor. Now here was one, come floating in from the sea, a piece of wrack to be carefully preserved for the good of all the island. Wrack came from heaven, and some of it was very strange. No one but a fool quarrels with his luck.

We reached Mamó's house at last, and knocked at her door. We knew that she was inside, by the red glow behind the curtains. This meant that she had heard no word about the wreck. If she had, she would have been down at Luke's house, with all the other women, listening to all the talk about it and saying what a terrible thing it was.

She opened the door in a moment, and stood there staring at us and at the man we still supported between us. In the light streaming from the door his face was as white as a seagull's wing.

"God save us all," she said after a moment. "Where did ye pick up that poor garlach?"

"Can we come in?" I asked.

"Of course, of course. Come in this minute. And sure, how can you, and I blocking the door."

She trotted into the kitchen to make way for us, and then she shut the door firmly. Mamó's house was like every house on the island. The door opened into the kitchen, where there was always a good turf fire. We have our own turf on Inishgillan, not like the Aran Islands, where the turf has to come over nine miles in boats from Connemara. Having our own turf makes us more generous with fires, and there was a fine one that evening that we brought the doctor into Mamó's house.

Two rooms opened off the kitchen, one behind the fire, where Mamó slept, and one at the other side where we knew she had a big bed always ready in case a visitor might come. I opened the door of this room.

"We'll put him on the bed," I said. "He's nearly dead from the walk."

"Let me get warm by the fire first," said the doctor in a hoarse voice. "It won't do me any harm to wait a few minutes more," he said, as I hesitated. "You can find some pieces of wood to make splints, and an old sheet to tear up for bandages."

It was true that he was stone cold, and we had not the heart to put him into the room at once. Mamó said:

"Splints? Has he broken bones? Where did ye find him?"

"I'll tell you in a minute."

I pretended that I had breath for nothing but helping the doctor over to the fire. Mamó pulled out the settle from the wall and we made him as comfortable as we could, lying against one end with his shoulders on a pillow, with his leg stretched out in front of him. He moaned when I lifted the broken leg onto the settle, so that I had to harden myself not to drop it.

"I'll get the wood for the splints," I said, and I made for the door.

Under cover of the tall back of the settle, I signalled to Mamó to come out with me. She turned to Roddy and said:

"Keep a good eye on him there for a minute while I show Patcheen where the timber is."

Once we were outside, we shut the door to keep the wind from roaring all round the kitchen. It was still as fierce as ever. I went around the corner of the house to shelter before I began to tell Mamó what had happened.

"A huge ship, grey and white, new like a cup or a picture—you never saw the like, sitting below on the black rocks, like a cart you'd have gathering weed—"

I hardly knew what I was saying, for it was only now I was beginning to feel the excitement of what had happened.

"And was this man on the big ship? How did he get ashore?"

"They lowered two boats. One got ashore with all the men. They're below at Luke's this minute, drinking tea, and maybe something else too."

"And the second boat?"

"It never came ashore, only Roddy and myself found this man crawling out of the sea when we went to take another look at the ship. 'Twas God sent him to us."

"'Tis God that sends us everything," she said.

"Yes, and now He has sent us a doctor, what we've wanted for years."

"A doctor? He's a doctor?"

"He said so."

She was silent for a moment, so that I didn't know what to expect. Then she said softly:

"It could be done. He'll need care and good food, if he's to get well. A dead doctor is no good to anyone."

"You'll keep him in the room?"

"He'll be glad to stay in that room for a while, I'm thinking," she said. "He doesn't feel too bad this evening. It's tomorrow he'll have a fever, and he'll be glad of a good bed."

"But he won't stay in bed for ever."

"We'll have time to think of that later."

We said no more about it while we went to the shed and found four short, flat pieces of wood. We brought these back into the kitchen, and I cut them into narrow pieces under the doctor's directions. Mamó got out an old sheet from the big chest by the fire, and she tore it into long narrow strips.

It was that evening that I discovered that I had a special gift for doctoring. Roddy had filled the kettle and hung it over the fire, as the doctor told him, and Mamó had helped with preparing the bandages, but Roddy was useless from that on.

When the kettle boiled, the doctor said to Roddy:

"Now take a basin of that water and wash your hands thoroughly with soap and then you can cut away the leg of my trousers from the broken bone—what's the matter with you?"

Roddy had backed away against the kitchen wall. His face was as white as the doctor's own, or rather, it was a yellowish, waxy colour because his skin is naturally sallow.

"Cut away the leg of your trousers? Don't ask me to do that!"

The doctor's eyes were narrow with rage, and his voice was a snarl.

"Would you like to put the bandage outside my trousers? Does that make sense to you? Or did you ever hear of germs?"

"I did. I heard of them. But I never had any dealings with them."

"Not only will you cut away the leg of my trousers, but you'll swab the wound with cloth sterilised with boiling water so that I won't die of gangrene, and then you'll bandage it as I tell you to do, fixing the splints in the way that I tell you."

"Ah, now, Doctor! Ah, now, Doctor!" Roddy was saying over and over during this speech, and backing harder and harder against the wall as if he would have liked to back out through it.

The doctor had a red blotch on his forehead, from

temper, and he was jerking about on the settle as if he could not lie still. This must have been very painful for him. I said:

"Keep quiet, or you'll fall on the floor. I'll do all those things for you. Lie back there quietly and tell me what to do."

He glared at me for a moment, and then said sourly:

"Very well. Two would have been better than one."

"Won't I do for the other one?" said Mamó indignantly.

It was she who got the basin of water, and handed me the splints one by one, and rolled the bandages, but she could not bring herself to look at the place on his leg where the bone had broken the skin, and the blood had dried all around the wound.

I found this very interesting, and I hardly needed the doctor's directions about placing the two parts of the bone together and bandaging them firmly so that they could not move. It was for all the world like mending the handle of a fork, or an oar. I said as much to the doctor, but he made no reply. I even whistled a little while I worked, because it somehow made me very contented, to find that I was so good at it. At last I said cheerfully:

"That's the best I can do. I have a new skill—"

As I tied the last knot on the bandage I looked up and saw the doctor had fainted again.

"That's a good job," I said to the others. "Now we can get him into bed. If he hadn't fainted before now, he'd have done it on the way into the room."

Roddy was able to help, of course, now that there was no more blood to be seen. We dragged the settle as near to the room door as we could. Then we lifted him between the three of us and carried him, and laid him awkwardly on the big bed. Mamó covered him with many blankets and her warmest quilt, and we put two boxes into the bed, one on either side, to keep the weight of the clothes off his injured leg. We left a candle lighting on the mantel-shelf, lest he should wake in fright, and then we went back to the kitchen to remove all traces of our evening's work and to hold a conference.

"There's no one need know he's there at all," said Mamó. "No one ever has any business to look into that room, except myself."

"You might have a visitor," I said.

"I'll watch out for them," said she, "and if I see anyone coming I'll take my shawl from behind the door, and I'll let on that I'm just going out visiting myself."

"If they come on you by surprise?"

"I'll keep the room door shut. That poor man won't be able to walk around for a while, by the looks of him."

"He might shout. He might call out, if he knew there was someone in the kitchen."

"He doesn't look a very sociable man to me," said Mamó. "I'm thinking it's trying to avoid people he'll be, instead of drawing them on him. Now tell me all about the wreck. You saw her banging on the rocks, God look down on us all!"

And she sat forward eagerly on the hob, to hear all about it. When we had described what we had seen, she said:

"If I don't go down to Luke's to hear all about it, maybe someone will think of coming up here for me, old Sally herself, maybe." Sally was Luke's mother, and she was not a day younger than Mamó, though she always called her "old Sally." She cocked an eye at us. "Two boys will never be missed. The two of ye can stay here till I get back. I won't be long."

But we knew by the way she banked up the fire with turf that she was going to stay while there was any fun going on. As she reached her shawl from the peg behind the door, I said softly:

"Be sure you don't say a word about the doctor, Mamó. If they give you a sweet drop below in Luke's, you might forget."

"I won't forget, agrá, no matter what they give me. I'll put that information in along with a few other secrets I have, in a special quarter of my brain, and there's no one living will get it out of me."

And she went off, with a springing step like a young girl.

Roddy laughed and said to me:

"She has that special place in her brain for secrets, all right. She won't tell. Remember the time the excise man came asking did anyone see the barrels of Scotch whisky, and she persuaded him to go over to Bofin for it."

"It's easier to hide a barrel of whiskey than a doctor," said I. "When he gets well enough to walk around— that's when the trouble will start."

"It's not as if we had a pier. We don't have visitors."

"We have the priest every Sunday, and Willie O'Connell with the post, and surely someone will come about the wreck—"

We were silent a long time, thinking about it. Every moment made it seem more and more impossible that we would be able to keep him, but as Roddy said at last, we could only go on until we had to give up.

"Time enough to think about giving up when we have to," he said.

It was eleven o'clock when Mamó came back. We had been in to have a look at the doctor several times, and he seemed to be asleep, breathing fast but regularly. Her first question was:

"How is he?"

"Not so bad. At least that's how he looks."

"We can do no more for him," said she impatiently. "Wait till I tell you the news! The rest of the men from the second boat were washed up a few yards away from where ye found the doctor. They're below in Luke's this minute!"

"All of them?"

"Every one. They counted. They're lamenting over the loss of the doctor. Big John and Bartley stayed below by the ship when the others went up to Luke's and they saw them, five of them, crawling in over the rocks the way ye saw the doctor. They were nearer to the slip than he was, however that happened."

"Any broken bones among them?"

"Sorro' one," said Mamó, "except a Spaniard with a broken finger on his left hand. He has it tied up handsome, and he looks like a cat in a tripe shop, because he'll get fine compensation from the owners of the ship. *Coriander*, her name is. Isn't it a lovely name? The *Coriander*. The others have cuts and bruises galore, but they're used to that. They don't feel them, hardly, they're so glad to be off the sea. They're all the time listening to the wind knocking at the door, as if they thought it was coming to get them."

On our way home we called in at Luke's. The kitchen was still full of people. It was easily the best kitchen on the island, being extra long and wide because once the post office business used to be carried on at one end of it.

Luke used to have the machine for sending messages in Morse, and the presses for the record books and stamps, and the scales for weighing parcels, as well as a counter to put them on, all together at the end farthest from the fireplace. Then an inspector came from the Department of Posts and Telegraphs and said that this would not do, that the money and the stamps must be kept in a locked room lest they be stolen. I can tell you that Luke's nightly visitors were not a bit pleased at this suggestion. Tomás Rua thought of ducking the inspector in the sea to teach him some manners. But when they found that Luke was getting a new room built on to his house, free, they said that that was another story. Everyone was very well pleased, not only because Luke had a bigger kitchen, but also because now he stayed with the company, chatting, instead of going back and forth to his desk as he had been accustomed to do before. The talk was always better when he was there.

It was nearly over when we arrived that evening. Luke was standing with his back to the fire, arranging where the shipwrecked sailors were to sleep. There were eleven of them, as well as the captain and the two officers. The captain was South American, with not a word of English or Irish to his name. He was a middle-aged man, rather tall, and broad like most South Americans. He sat looking straight in front of him, and now and then a single tear would roll down his face. It went through my heart to see a grown man in such a state, though I knew I would have been the same if I had lost the *Coriander*.

One of the sailors who spoke English and Spanish explained to us:

"He thinks he should still be on the ship, that that is the captain's place. But we made him come with us when we saw that the ship was lost. He did everything that any man could do. Now he is crying for his ship, and also for his great friend the doctor, who is lost too."

"The doctor?" said Roddy innocently.

"Yes, yes, we had a doctor," said the man. "He and the captain used to play chess every evening and tell each other stories—oh, they were great friends. And now the doctor is dead and drowned, and the poor captain weeps for him and for the *Coriander*."

"Perhaps the doctor was washed ashore with the rest of you," I said uncomfortably, for I was always a poor hand at lying. "Perhaps he'll turn up later on."

The sailor looked at me with contempt and said:

"You don't know what you're talking about. We were in the boat. The doctor was swept out by a wave long, long before the boat overturned. He is lost away out, yards out from the shore. Our boat did not capsize until she was quite near in. I know what *I'm* talking about. If he turns up later on he will be dead."

I was glad that Luke called him away just then, to tell him that Tomás Rua had a bed for him. All the men began to shuffle out, leading their charges. We went out in the crowd, so as to be forgotten among them, for that sailor had raised his voice and drawn some attention to us.

Luke's wife Molly had her eye on us. I never cared for her, since the time she caught me with my pockets full of stones to chase her old goat out of our cabbage field. She was a plague to us, that goat, and I was watching her edging her way into the field for half an hour, giving an eye at the house every second minute to see was anyone there. I was behind the cart shelter and I had the stones all ready to let fly and teach her a lesson she would not forget in a hurry, when Molly saw me and came running in to rescue the goat. Molly couldn't prove that the stones in my pocket were for the goat, but never afterwards would she let me listen to the music that came over the post office earphones. I didn't want her to come over now and start asking me what the sailor had said. She is too clever, and she might have asked a lot of questions not easily answered.

That night I gave my bed willingly to another sailor, and slept in the kitchen settle bed. I always loved to do this, to watch the fire sink lower and lower, until the brown ash covered it quite over, and to feel the house go quieter as the people in it fell asleep one by one. That night the wind was noisy, shaking the four corners of the house every few minutes and rustling in the thatch, but still I felt a difference in the air when there was no one awake but myself. I began to wonder how the *Coriander* was getting on, and I could not keep out of the back of my mind a hope that the night's gale would finish her. I fell asleep, dreaming of sacks of her cargo being washed into every cove of the shore of Inishgillan, as well as portholes and doors and ladders and coils of rope, and all the wonderful things that go to keep a ship together.

The next morning, Roddy and I met early, down by the slip. There was a crowd there already when we arrived. The sea was still wild, green and grey and white, pockmarked all over by the wind. The edge of it was a rolling, roaring mass of spray and foam that would chew up a currach and swallow it in a minute. The men were silent, watching the *Coriander*. I knew how they felt, helpless and angry because there was no question of getting near her where she was perched on the jagged teeth of the rocks. One or two of the sailors were there too, but they seemed to be not so much interested in the wreck as in the geography of Inishgillan. The same man came over to us, the one who had spoken to us the evening before.

"This is a wild place," he said rudely. "How long will it be before we get back to civilisation?"

"Not too long, I hope," said I. "You'll have to go in the lifeboat, and they won't come for you until the sea goes down a bit."

"What's up there?"

"Nothing much," I said casually, though my heart was pounding with fear that he might take a walk up as far as Mamó's house and drop in for a chat, or perhaps peek in through the window and see the doctor. "Nothing but cliffs. The wind is stronger up there than it is down here."

He laughed sourly.

"What a country! Does anyone ever get blown off those cliffs?"

"Sometimes strangers do."

He laughed again, as if he were pleased to find that I was as sour as himself.

The *Coriander* was no longer as firmly fixed as she had been last night. Every few minutes she lifted herself up heavily and came down again. We guessed that she was holed below the water-line, and it was terrible to think of the sea water flowing in and out through the hole, and soaking the cargo that we already considered ours.

Sidecar trotted up to Luke and said:

"Can't you send for the lifeboat, Luke agrá? Can't you send them a message on the telegraph to say the men are waiting to go to Galway? There's a man with a broken finger, wanting attention from a doctor. There's the other men, that were washed in and out with the tide, and you'll tell the lifeboat men to hurry, Luke, or the ship will be broken up before we get all the lovely things off her!"

"Ssh! Ssh" Luke pushed Sidecar away from the others to read him a lecture on keeping his tongue quiet. Then he set off up the road towards the post office, apparently to take Sidecar's advice.

Roddy and I went up to Mamó's house. No one was working today. There was not much we could do in this weather in any case, but even if there had been, it would have been neglected for watching the *Coriander*. We took the precaution of going around by the lower path, past the ship, as we had done when we were taking the doctor up to Mamó's the evening before. There was nothing strange in our visiting Mamó. We just did not want people to think of her at all, lest they might begin to wonder what was keeping her at home on such a day.

She welcomed us anxiously when we arrived, and brought us in at once to look at the doctor.

"The poor man is not right in the head today," she said. "He's imagining all sorts of things. I wonder are we doing murder between us?"

"How do you mean?"

"Keeping him here instead of sending him in to Galway in the lifeboat."

We stood looking down at him. It was a horrible thought. Then Roddy said:

"How do we know but that the journey into Galway would kill him? It's a long way on a rough sea, for a man with a broken leg."

"He's so hot, the creature," said Mamó, "and he's ramaishing about knights and bishops and kings—I wonder what kind of company does he be in when he's at home."

We stayed with him for a while, to let Mamó go down to the slip. We did not sit in the bedroom, because the low, husky voice rambling on in a confidential way got on our nerves. His eyes were shut, and his hands wandering about the bedclothes were like the hands of a blind man feeling for something he has lost. We watched him silently for a few minutes, and then we went out to sit in the kitchen. We shut the door between, in case anyone would drop in, though we knew that this was unlikely.

"It's a good thing he's keeping his voice low," I said. "If he were shouting, we'd have the whole island in on top of us."

"I wonder should you take the bandage off his leg and have a look at it?" Roddy said after a long pause.

I guessed that the notion did not please him, but that his conscience made him suggest it. He looked relieved when I said:

"No, it would be like lifting the earth off the sciolláns in the springtime, to see if they were sprouting. It's better to leave it alone."

We got down Mamó's pack of cards from the mantel and played a game of twenty-five, but we hardly knew who was winning. Every time a hen trotted up to the door, we jumped in our skins. Our ears were sore from trying to hear someone coming, above the roar of the wind. And yet, when Mamó came back, she was right in the kitchen before we heard her.

"Luke telegraphed for the lifeboat," she said, "but they're afraid to come today. There's a ship aground off Mutton Island, imagine it, right inside in Galway Bay.

That must have been a wind! 'Tis no wonder it ran the *Coriander* ashore, as I've told the captain below, but he made me no answer."

"You should have said it in Spanish," said Roddy.

That night the shipwrecked sailors were still billeted in different houses, but they gathered at Luke's in the evening as if they were going to have a dance. The only difference was in their sad faces. They did not like our island, and those that had English told us so, and told us why. In every house, a special meal had been cooked for the strangers. Some had a piece of bacon, boiled with cabbage, and a big pot of potatoes. Some had salt ling, a long, flat fish that we keep stored until we need it, and a big pot of potatoes. And some had captured a veteran hen that was past laying, and boiled her with cabbage, and with her they had a big pot of potatoes.

"If the lifeboat were to come for us now, we'd sink it," said the sour sailor who had talked with me in the morning. "Don't you ever eat anything but potatoes, potatoes, potatoes?"

"Oh, yes," I said solemnly. "We grow asparagus and grapes, and alfalfa. We're very fond of the alfalfa."

These words I had from my uncle in western America. All I knew about them was that they grew in the ground. The sailor glared at me, and muttered in his own language. My father came across the kitchen and said peaceably:

"Tomorrow the lifeboat will come. Let ye all be happy since there's no more ye can do about it. Strike up an old song there, till we hear what kind of music ye have in those places."

But not a bar would they sing for us. They went home to bed early. Suddenly I found that I could hardly keep myself awake. The island men sat in their places without moving, each man talking earnestly to the man beside him. The air was blue with tobacco smoke, and with the puffs of smoke that the wind sent down the chimney from time to time. Though I found it hard to leave their company, I said good night to Luke and Molly, and went off to my own house next door.

My mother had left Luke's house half an hour before me. When I came in she said:

"Any sign of your father coming home?"

"Not a move from any of them," I said. "They're like they grew in the chairs. And they're chatting away so happily between themselves, you'd think they hadn't met for a month."

"The wind is down a bit," she said. "I'd say the lifeboat will be here tomorrow."

"Please God it will," I said, thinking of our unwilling guests.

Some time during the night the storm blew off to the west. I awoke to a strange stillness. A wide bar of sunlight was lying on the kitchen floor, showing that the house door was open. I sprang off the settle. There was no one in the kitchen, no one in the house buy myself. I threw on a few clothes and ran outside, and climbed the wall that keeps our little garden from being nibbled at by every passing donkey. Standing on the flat stones there, I looked towards the sea. It lay almost calmly, a whitish grey reflecting the winter sun, with a white line of foam at the edge from the groundswell. One look showed me enough to send me leaping off the wall and darting like a hare down the road to the slip.

I found my mother at once.

"Why didn't you wake me?"

"You were sleeping like a log. I left the door open so you'd know we were gone."

Everyone was there, watching the lifeboat sliding up and down the waves as she made for the shore. The sailors stood in a little group on the slip, as near to the sea as they could go without wetting their boots. I took all this in at a glance, and at the same moment I saw that the *Coriander* was gone. I looked quickly at the island men, standing in a group apart from the sailors. Their eyes were dancing with delight, and every man had a huge, uncontrollable grin on his face. Big John Moran was rolling up and down from his heels to his toes and back again. I went over to him.

"The *Coriander* is gone," I said in a low voice.

"She's gone, for sure," said he.

And he laughed happily.

"What happened to her?"

"Some time in the night, the sea lifted her off the rocks, and took her out a little piece, and she drifted along to Trá Fhada, and she's there this minute, out of sight and out of harm's way."

"Will she be salvaged?"

"No, by the mercy of God, she's beyond salvaging."

I knew she was safe then, for when Big John talked about God, times were usually very good. I felt myself grinning like everyone else, and when the sailors got aboard the lifeboat, the contrast between their glum faces and our cheerful ones was so strong that Willie O'Connell of the lifeboat remarked on it:

"You're looking very happy, Big John. Aren't you sorry for these unfortunate men that lost their ship?"

"Sorry I am indeed for that," said Big John, "but glad that they're alive."

"All except the doctor," said the sailor who had spoken to me on their first evening on the island.

"Ah, I forgot about the doctor," said Big John, and he shook the captain's hand very seriously and wished him a safe journey.

By Willie's hard looks at us, I could see that he guessed we were expecting a great haul from the *Coriander*, but he said nothing. Out at sea, the sailors waved to us once, and then turned their backs on us and our island, thankfully, as we knew.

That was a great day. Neither Roddy nor I dared to ask how the *Coriander* had reached the shelter of the cove at Trá Fhada. No one would answer a boy's question on a subject like that. All we knew was that she was there, and that the currachs and their oars were wet, and that the men were so tired in the evening that they all went to bed at eight o'clock and slept till eight the next morning. We had to help with unloading the ship through most of the day and it was not until evening that we were set free to go up to Mamó's house.

"I'm waiting for ye all day," she said crossly. "I was afraid to go out and leave the doctor. Only that I went out to the road to talk to Sally, I wouldn't know what's after happening with the *Coriander*."

"We couldn't stir," Roddy said. "We've been working like donkeys since the lifeboat went."

"How is he?" I asked.

"That's our trouble," she said. "He's getting better. He's asking about the captain and the ship. He's wanting to know who's saved besides himself. I had to let on to be a bit foolish so that I wouldn't have to answer him. I said you'd be up this evening to talk to him, and that he should content himself until then. Let you go in now, so that he'll be quiet for the evening."

You may be sure that I was not anxious to go in. But

it was no use putting it off, and I had to face the result of our decision to kidnap him. If it was ever discovered that we had kept him in Inishgillan against his will, I would be in prison for the rest of my life. It was not much comfort to know that Roddy would probably be with me.

Chapter Three

The doctor had hauled himself up in bed, and was lying against a huge pile of pillows. I noticed that these were covered with Mamó's best embroidered pillow-cases, that she was keeping for her own wake. She had been trying to compensate him, I suppose, for the injury that we were doing him. I thought his peevish face looked very strange against the flowers and birds of the embroidery. His eyes were fixed on the door and he snapped at us the moment that we appeared:

"Come in, come in. I thought you'd never come. I could get no sense out of the old woman. Tell me, what's the news of the ship? Who else got ashore? The people in my boat, and in the other boat, where are they?"

"You remember that?" I said slowly, to give myself time to think.

"Of course I remember it. And I remember your clumsy hands on my leg. I want a doctor, and quickly. I can't reach the place myself, and in any case, all my drugs are on the ship. Did she run aground? Perhaps you could get them for me."

He turned to Roddy.

"You, boy! You look more intelligent." He stopped and gazed at Roddy. "No, you're the one that refused to cut away the leg of my trousers. Oh, yes. I remember everything. Now, quickly, if you please. Was the ship saved?"

"In a manner of speaking."

He glared at us.

"And the men? And the captain?"

I glanced sideways at Roddy but there was no help coming from him. There was no way of breaking my news gently. The only comfort was in the knowledge that the doctor was helpless and that I could run out of the room, out of the house, at any moment that I wanted, while he had to stay immovable in the bed. Still I could not bring myself to look at him as I answered:

"The Inishbofin lifeboat came this morning and took away the captain and all the men. They're all safe."

He was silent for a minute while he tried to understand this. I felt myself go redder with every moment. At last he said:

"They're gone? They've left the island?"

"Yes," I said, as if I were talking to an idiot. "In the lifeboat."

He laid the palms of his hands flat on the quilt.

"And did you tell them about me?"

"No."

His voice was quiet, but quivering with fury.

"Why not? I had told you I wanted to go to Galway."

Roddy came to life.

"You did not, sir. You never said a word about Galway."

"Quiet, you!" He turned back to me. "Now, why did you not tell the captain I was here? Why did he not come to see me? Why did he just leave the island in the lifeboat, and never think of me?"

"He thought of you, all right. He thought you were drowned. He was very sorry about it."

"And you didn't tell him that I am not drowned? Why?"

There was no avoiding the question any longer. Through the open door I could hear the murmur of Mamó's voice, saying her prayers. I knew she was praying for me, but it did not seem to make my task any easier.

"We want to keep you here," I said in a low voice. "We need a doctor on the island, this many a year. We're sick and tired from asking for one, and he never comes. There's people dying every year for want of a doctor— "

"I don't believe it." His voice cut through what I was saying, so sharp that I jumped and bit my tongue. He observed this and it seemed to please him. "How many people do you remember seeing die for lack of a doctor?"

"They have to go in the lifeboat to Galway," I said. "It's very bad for them. 'Tis a long journey if you're sick, to be crossing the ocean holding yourself together, hoping that you'll get into Galway alive."

"Do they die?"

"No," I said sulkily. "No one did yet anyway but we're not waiting until they do."

"So I'm your prisoner, then?"

"In a manner of speaking."

Again he stared at us. I could see that he was not accustomed to finding himself in difficulties of any kind. He had the look of a man that is always able to dominate his company, whose words are enough to send people hurrying to obey him. He tried this way out now, by ordering me to go to the post office at once, and instruct the lifeboat men to come back and fetch him.

"No," I said. "We have made up our minds. You're going to stay here. So you'd best learn to content yourself."

This sounded so brave that it gave me courage.

"And shouting would be bad for your leg," I went on. "A man with a broken leg must keep very quiet. Anyway, this is a far, quiet house, and there's no one will hear you."

At that point I found that I could say no more, and I hustled Roddy before me into the kitchen. I shut the door quietly, with one glance back at the doctor. His eyes were bright and hard, like the eyes of a man about to do murder. His jaw stuck out wickedly, and even though I knew he could not move, I would not have gone a step nearer to him for Ireland free, no more than I would go into a tiger's cage.

"God bless my soul!" I said to Mamó when I was safe in the kitchen. "That's one cross man."

"You told him?"

"I did, sure. He looked like he had a mind to bite off our heads. But he won't mind you, because he really thinks you are a bit simple. You played your part well!"

This I said because it occurred to me suddenly that if Mamó got frightened, we would be in real difficulty about how to look after him. If she became afraid of bringing him his meals, for instance, one of us would have to do it. Too many visits to Mamó's house would not pass unnoticed.

We had to promise Mamó that we would come at certain times of the day, so that she could go out. That evening we had to stay in her kitchen while she went down to Luke's. It was the first of many vigils, and within a few days we both knew that we were never intended to be jailers. We used to get sorry for the doctor, and we were mortally afraid of doing him some harm from which he would never recover. He noticed this, and he played on it shamelessly.

As soon as Mamó had her shawl on, she would always put her head around the door and say to him:

"I'm off out for an airing. Let you lie there nice and comfortable until I come back, and the boys will look after you."

She would be gone no further than the road when he would start calling for a drink of water, or to have his dressing changed or his pillows fixed. This we dreaded especially, because while we leaned in over him to do it he would nip us unmercifully through our jerseys. If we did not come quickly enough for his liking, he would start shouting and whistling and banging on the bed-head. This always brought us running. It was true what we had told him, that the house was remote and quiet, but sometimes a man would pass by on his way to look at young cattle higher up on the island, or one of Mamó's friends would drop in for a moment to see if she was there. This only happened once or twice, because the wreck was keeping everyone busy. At any other time, Mamó's kitchen was hardly ever without an old woman sitting on the hob warming herself, getting on with her knitting and swapping news. The couple of times that they came while the doctor was in bed, by good luck he happened to have fallen asleep.

In two or three days the wind dropped, and we had calm, white winter weather. The sea shone like satin, and little waves flowed gently in and out, rattling the coloured shells on the shore. We were like seagulls clustering on a dead shark around the *Coriander*. Apart from the cargo in the hold, portholes, stairways, banisters—everything came out, as well as the furniture from the passengers' and the officers' quarters and the pots and crockery from the galley.

A great deal of the crockery was broken, of course, and we did not much care for what was there, it was so plain. All our women like cups and dishes with flowers, especially roses. The ship's cups were plain white. I thought that if I owned a ship, I would have cups and plates with every kind of old ship painted on them, barques and brigantines and galleons in full sail. But the captain of the *Coriander* was not her owner at all, and he probably had little choice in what went into her.

Roddy and I found the doctor's cabin. We knew it by the size of the suits hanging in the wardrobe, long, thin suits, so like himself that we were nearly afraid to touch them. We found a beautiful polished wooden box full of bottles and pills, and a leather case of knives and scissors of various sizes. We made sure to get these things into our own currach, and when we got them ashore, we hid them among the rocks instead of sending them off with all the other things. In the excitement, no one noticed what we were doing.

With rope ladders hanging over the *Coriander's* sides, the men filled the currachs and brought all the wonderful things ashore. We have places for hiding things of this kind, but never in the history of the island did we have a haul like this one. A sack of flour, a few baulks of timber, bales of rubber or roofing felt—that was the sort of thing we were used to. Sometimes a cabin door would come drifting in from a wreck, and the man that found it would use it in his house at once, without fear. But cargo was supposed to be handed over to the revenue officers, a foolish old idea, as we thought. We usually brought it to one of the deep, dry caves beyond Trá Fhada, and the man who had found it drew on it from time to time until it was finished.

Big John Moran superintended the unloading. When the things were landed on the beach, donkey carts took them away to the caves where my father and Bartley MacDonagh stored them safely. When darkness fell, we beached our currachs and carried them ashore, and laid them safely upside down in sheltered places. Then we swung up the road to the shop, where all the men had a fine pint of black porter before going home to eat.

On the third day, when the last of the unloading was finished, the crowd of men was especially cheerful.

"'Tis like the answer to the Maiden's Prayer," said Sidecar. "We'll never see a poor day again."

My father and Bartley had dropped behind, and they signalled to me to come and walk with them.

"Tell Big John we want to have a word with him," my father said, "but tell him quietly so that the rest won't hear you."

I ran ahead and got in beside Big John. He was rather quiet this evening, and I supposed it was the days of hard work that had tired him. I whispered my message to him, and he dropped out at once and waited for the other two to come up with him.

"What's troubling you?" he said anxiously when he saw my father's face.

"All that stuff off the ship. There's too much of it there. If we keep it, we'll never see God. It would be thieving and stealing in the highest degree."

"That has been my own thought for the last day," said Big John. "Were you at the caves? They're packed as tight as Máirtín Mór MacDonagh's warehouse in Galway."

The most exciting part of the cargo for us was the large number of cardboard boxes filled with navy-blue suits of clothes. This is the colour we all love best, a decent colour, and one that a man feels well in. Some of the boxes were opened on the strand and the cloth tested by many fingers. Everyone agreed that it was of the finest quality and that the making was a credit to the tailors of South America.

But now Bartley said:

"'Tis the suits of clothes are troubling me most. There's one there for every man on the island, and for every man's son, and his grandson too, if he had one. And I'm even thinking there's more than one, that there's two or three suits for every man. How do we know we'd live to wear them out? 'Tis a terrible thing to have two suits."

"There's lovely cloth in them," my father said wistfully. "But I was thinking of them too. If I was wearing one of those suits, when it would get a bit old maybe, and if I was to see Willie O'Connell making in towards the slip, I'd start and I'd run home, and I'd get back into the old bréidín before he'd see me. I know that for certain sure. And doesn't that mean that I'd feel 'twasn't honest to be wearing it?"

"Ay, that's so," said the other two. "'Tis so, indeed."

"What will we do then?" asked Big John. "'Twould go against my grain to send for the Revenue Men."

"And against mine," said my father. "But there's this to be said for sending for them: that we would know when they would be coming."

"That's so," the others agreed.

You may be sure that Roddy and I were listening

closely to this conversation. We were thinking of the doctor. He would not stay in bed for ever. When he would be well again, the difficulties of keeping him hidden would be multiplied. If the Revenue Men were to come without warning, they would be all over the island, poking into every house to see if there was anything there off the *Coriander*. It would be next to impossible to hide him. We knew, of course, that we would have to tell our own people that we had such a valuable prisoner, but we wanted to pick our own time for this. They say that the battle goes with the general that fires the first shot.

At the shop, the men crowded in and sat down, or as many of them sat as could find stools. Andy Folan had a new barrel tapped. When every man had a glass in his hand, Big John stood up and looked them over. He could see, as I could, that they had begun to think about the *Coriander*, and that their thoughts were making them uneasy. But it was a long time before he was able to persuade them that at least some of the cargo would have to be sent into Galway. He had to face a battery of growls.

"Findings is keepings."

"'Twas God sent the *Coriander*."

"God helps those that help themselves."

"What do we care for their Revenue Men or their Guards?"

"What do they do for us? We keep our own law and order on Inishgillan."

"If they send the army and navy, we'll fight them both."

"We can stand a siege for a year and a day."

"A wreck is for all comers. 'Tis the bounty of the sea."

"But it wasn't a wreck," said Big John quickly.

"And what was it?"

"'Twas a ship aground. We floated it off the rocks and took it around to Trá Fhada. If we had left it here, it might have stayed high and dry, to be salvaged, if no storm came up."

"If! If! Sure, doesn't a storm always come up?"

We kept very quiet and out of sight as far as we could. If anyone had seen us or noticed us, we should have been sent home immediately. Big John said:

"It's a flat calm now, and it looks like it will be so for the next few days."

"But after that? After that?"

"All right, all right. After that the ship would be broken up. It would for certain sure. There would never be time in the winter to salvage her, not in this place."

"Now you're talking sense. Now you're seeing reason," said all the growlers.

"So it might be right to keep the ship and her fittings. But there would have been time, and more than time, for boats to come out from Galway and take in her cargo, if Luke had telegraphed the first day, or if Willie O'Connell had seen the *Coriander* and had sent out the boats. But we hid her, and we have no moral right to that cargo."

There was a short silence. Then one man said:

"If Willie had seen the *Coriander* and had sent out boats from Galway, there might have been a storm."

But it was a half-hearted protest. The storm had died down, no thanks to us, and the men that had moved the *Coriander* had known that this would happen.

"Very well," they said at last. "Let Big John make all the arrangements. But I'm thinking 'twill be a long time before the sea will send us anything again."

We slipped outside without being seen, and walked briskly through the cold night air to Mamó's house. I said:

"If they knew the one-half of what the sea has sent us!"

We told Mamó quickly what had happened, and advised her to go down to the shop at once and hear what was being planned.

"They were right excited," said Roddy. "They never looked to see who was listening, before talking of how they saved the *Coriander*. There's one sight I wish I had seen, all the currachs harnessed to the ship by ropes, and they pulling and towing her up to Trá Fhada. 'Tis a thing that may never happen again in my lifetime."

Big John waited until the next day before sending for the Revenue Men. He wanted to sleep on it, he said, to make sure he was doing the right thing. I was at Luke's in the morning when he came in to talk about it.

"We'll need time to bring the cargo from the caves over here," he said. "You're a Government official, Luke, being the Postmaster. 'Twould be proper to store it in your sheds. The Revenue Men will be happy when they see it there. We can let on that we brought it here direct from the ship."

"Do you think that they'll go searching around the island?" I asked.

"Why should they? They'll get so much here that they'll be satisfied. What would bring them poking around the island?"

"One of them is Jack O'Brien's son, from Inishthorav."

Inishthorav is the next island to ours, between us and Inishbofin. Five miles of stormy water separate us, enough, you'd think, to make it hard for us to quarrel with each other. But it was not enough. There was a feud as old as the seven hills of Rome between our two islands. It broke out into blows from time to time, and the most recent fight was after the great currach races in Galway. Usually that sort of fight is over the question of who is the winner of the race. That was not the way with us. Before the race had time to start at all, before the first blade of the first oar struck the water, Mike Rua from Inishthorav looked over at the currach of Tomás Rua of Inishgillan beside him and shouted out:

"Wrecker!"

There was an old story among the Inishthorav men, that Tomás Rua's grandfather, when he was a young man, had put out the Killaney light and had placed a light at the cliff top so as to wreck an outward bound ship from Galway. If the story was true, it had not made the grandfather rich, or if it had, he had spent his money long before Tomás came along. One way or another, Tomás broke out in a storm of fury and he aimed a blow at the Inishthorav currach with a mind to sink it. It was a terrible sight, the two red-haired men facing each other with eyes of murder, and the currachs rocking like mad on the waves. The steward's boat came steaming over and the two heroes were told that they would be put out of the race if there was any fighting. As luck would have it, the Inishgillan boat won the race, and if the Inishthorav men had small love for us before, they had less now.

"Jacko's son is a Revenue Man, sure enough," said Big John thoughtfully. "'Tis a complication. But 'tis not insurmountable."

"What will you do?"

"We'll send for them when the next storm is on its way, but before the weather men get to know about it."

Luke laughed delightedly. Big John could always foretell a storm well in advance of the weather men, by various small signs like the movements of the seagulls, and the porpoises, and the stormy petrels, and by the position of certain clouds. In the days before the islands had the radio, this skill had saved many a boat that might have gone out on a good sea, and got caught by the storm, and come home no more.

"They'll hurry with their business, sure enough, when they feel the storm coming," said Luke. "If there's one thing those boyoes hate, it's to be caught out on one of the islands by a storm. They do risk their necks every winter to get home out of the islands."

"Wouldn't you think they'd like a few quiet days on an island, playing cards every evening with the men, with no work, only strolling about pleasing themselves?" I said.

"I used to hear the men talking about it when I was on the ships," said Big John. "It seems you have to be born on an island to be able to live there. They feel shut in, they say, and they start worrying because they can't get off it."

"Where would they want to go?" I said in wonder. "And how could you feel shut in? You can nearly see America from the top of the island."

"And of course," said Big John, "they have an idea that the islanders do be laughing at them and making game of them. 'Tis true for them too, but there's to be no laughing this time, because we don't want to make them suspicious."

The weather continued calm for three days more, and the air was light and dry. The men were angry at having to spend time in bringing the cargo up to the post office but they had agreed to do it, and they worked hard at it every afternoon. Besides, they really had time to spare, because the spring planting had not yet begun. The road from the slip up to the post office was loud with the clatter of donkey carts. We were very uneasy during those days, because Big John passed by Mamó's door twice a day, on his way up to look out over the sea. He would surely have dropped in for a chat with Mamó if we had not kept a watch for him, and sent her down to meet him each time. A hundred yards below her own house, she would trot past him saying:

"The blessing of God on you, Big John! I'm just taking a run down to see the lovely things off the ship. Oh, Lord of the world! Isn't it a disgrace to be sending them away!"

And Big John would answer something like:

"Wasn't it you that taught me right from wrong, and I only knee-high to a puddle duck?"

And he would labour on up the hill, chuckling to himself. There he would stand for perhaps half an hour, gazing out to sea in every direction, seeming not to feel the cold that was still, in the middle of January, like the bite of a dog. Then he would walk down the hill again, past Mamó's shut door, and never know that we were peering at him from behind the kitchen curtains.

On the fourth morning he stayed up on the cliff no more than five minutes. We saw him hurry past. Roddy said to me:

"I'll stay with the old rasper inside while you go down and find out what's after happening. We can't go on like this much longer. The time we've wasted up here! Every island should have a jail—"

I ran off and left him grumbling. He had reason to grumble, because his family was beginning to ask him was he taking up schooling again, or why was he spending so much time up in Mamó's house. One of these days, someone would get wind of a secret and come up to have a look. If that were to happen while there were strangers on the island, there would be little hope for us.

Big John walked fast, but he was four times my age, and I got to Luke's house long before him. Luke's wife, Molly, was there at the door, looking down the hill to where the last of the donkey carts was toiling up with its load. Most of the things had been moved the evening before, but a few loads had remained when darkness fell, and they were being carted from the cave this morning. Molly looked quite cheerful, though her kitchen was crammed full of bales of all sorts. The sheds had not been big enough to hold everything. Not many women would be so patient.

"I'm thinking we're only just in time, Patcheen," she said to me, forgetting in her excitement that we were at war.

"Big John is on his way down, sure enough," I said.

She went out to the road wall, and put her head back, and let out a long piercing call like a dozen seagulls after a shoal of fish. Immediately, at every door all up and down the road, a woman appeared. Each took one look at Molly, then ran into her house for a moment and out again, and came running towards the post office. One had taken the pot off the fire, I suppose; one had put the baby back in the cradle; one had rubbed the flour off her hands; one had grabbed her little head-shawl for the sake of decency. Here they came, their red petticoats whirling and their blue-checked aprons tossing on the wind, and a chattering going on among them so that you would think they were a flock of strange birds.

When Big John rounded the bend in the road, he found that he had an audience waiting for him. The men had heard Molly's looring too, but they got there more slowly than the women, because they had to climb out of the little fields over loose stone walls. Some had to cross several fields before reaching the road.

"The storm is coming," said Big John. "There's a dark blue patch on the sea, and a dark blue cloud in the sky above it. The storm is there, for certain sure, like a hand in a pocket. Where is Luke?"

He was at Big John's side by this time.

"You're sure 'tis coming this way?" he asked, peering anxiously at the two dark specks.

These were so small that it would take an expert to see them, and especially to estimate what they meant.

"I am sure," said Big John, "unless the wind does something it never did before, and that's something that would not surprise me." He turned to the listening crowd: "Now, when the Revenue Men come, remember that they are Irishmen like ourselves. They have wives and little children at home. We have a reputation for hospitality on Inishgillan, so I've heard, and let ye all make sure that no visitor goes home today with a bad opinion of us. Tomorrow, I mean. Because they must stay for the night."

A murmuring began among the people, and it did not sound very hospitable to me. Big John said:

"Of course they must stay the night on the island. There's six hours, nearly, to come out from Galway, and then the cargo to be put on their ship. That will be slow. If they don't have to stay two nights, we'll be lucky."

"But the storm! That storm you see coming! If it comes before tomorrow night, they might be here for a month. Ochón ó! The poking they could do in a month!"

"That storm won't be as far as Inishgillan until tomorrow night," said Big John positively. "That will give us grand time to load them and send them off in a hurry about noon."

"'Tis tight measuring," said my father.

"Isn't that the way ye wanted it? Tight measuring is the only thing that will get them off fast. Now, Luke! In with you and get them started on their way."

Luke disappeared into the post office, and we could hear him tap-tap-tapping on his little machine, in the strange language that the post office people use.

All at once I guessed what was going to happen. There was no time for explanations. As quietly as I could, I went here and there among the crowd until I found Mamó. She was gossiping with her friend Sally. They had got tired of standing, and they were resting their old bones, sitting on the flat stones that decorated the front of Sally's house, which was just opposite Luke's. From there they had a fine view of what was happening.

I squatted beside Mamó and pulled at her skirt. When she turned to me a little, I said urgently:

"Go on away home, Mamó, as quick as you can!"

I was relying on Sally's deafness, that she would not overhear me.

"Why?" Mamó said in a low voice. "Why would I go home, agrá, and leave all the fun going on here?"

"Don't ask me now," I said desperately. "Just go on home now, before anyone says a word to you."

She gave me a sharp look, and then she heaved herself to her feet and trotted off, making her way around the edge of the crowd with such a preoccupied air that no one asked her where she was going.

Old Sally was prodding me with a hard, bony finger.

"Where is she gone?" she demanded. "What did you say to her, that made her get up and run off like that, without by your leave?"

"Her pig is in the cabbage field," I said desperately, and I regretted it immediately.

"So that's what boys are nowadays! You see her pig in the cabbage field, and you just say: 'Oh, there's Mamó's pig in the cabbage field.' And you walk down here, nice and slow, and tell that poor old woman that misfortune has struck her, and you leave her to run off up the hill herself to catch him and put him out of it. Mamó that taught you in school! I know what's good for you!"

I was listening to all this like one in a trance, when suddenly I saw her lift her fist. I ducked away from her, with my ears hot from her words and from the box that had nearly reached the one nearest to her. Old women are as fierce as geese, I said to myself.

I had been just in time. Big John was standing on Luke's doorstep now, with his hands spread out for silence. Gradually everyone stopped talking.

"Now, as I was saying, we're going to treat the Revenue Men to the height of hospitality," he said. "There will be four of them as well as the crew of the ship, but the crew can stay on the ship, of course. The Revenue Men must be given beds in our houses for the night. Two can stay here with Luke and Molly. That's only right and proper. And the other two—Mamó! Where's Mamó? The other two can stay with Mamó. She has a fine big bed, and she's the best able to talk to fine gentlemen like those. Where is she at all?"

"I saw her going off towards her own house about five minutes ago," said Bartley MacDonagh.

"The pig is in her cabbage garden," shouted old Sally, but no one took any notice of her.

I said:

"I'll go up after her and give her the message."

"Good boy," said Big John. "She can get out her best for them, tell her from me."

"I'll go this minute," I said, and I ran like a red-shank up the hill, signalling to Roddy to follow me.

We were glad to leave that crowd behind, but what was before us was even worse. All sorts of wild thoughts ran through my mind. We could bring the doctor to the caves and hide him there with the rest of the ship's goods. But no one except the island people knew the whereabouts of those caves, and it would be madness to show them to a stranger. Besides, the January cold would probably kill him. As Mamó had said, a dead doctor would not be much use to us, but apart from that, I was beginning to get quite fond of him, for all his sharp ways, as I had heard people get fond of a cross baby. Another thought that occurred to me was that we could dress him up in a trousers of the island bréidín, with a heavy knitted jersey, and force him to pretend he was one of ourselves. But if any of the Revenue Men were to hear him speak, there would be an end to our trick.

I poured out these ideas to Mamó the moment that I ran into the kitchen, panting. She said impatiently:

"What are you talking about? Isn't he safe here with me? Sure, nothing could happen him now, after all our trouble."

"Big John says you must have two of the Revenue Men here, to sleep in that very bed that the doctor is in," I said.

She paused for a moment to think, and then she said firmly:

"If that's the way of it, then the time has come to tell Big John that we have the doctor here."

Chapter Four

We gazed at Mamó in horror. All our trouble would be wasted, our careful piloting of the doctor around the side of Inishgillan that first evening, dragging his broken leg after him, and all our care of him since. I could find no words for a moment, and then I said slowly:

"Very well. That's the end of him. Now we'll never have a doctor on this island. Big John is too honest. He'll send him away with the Revenue Men, just as he's doing with the beautiful suits. He'll say he knows right from wrong—"

"Well, what else can we do?" Mamó demanded, and I saw now that her eyes were full of tears. I had never thought of her as a woman before, still less as a frightened old woman who was no more sure of her ground than I was myself. She said again, when neither Roddy nor I replied: "What else can we do? He's still a very sick man. He's talking of getting up, but even if he does, it will be a while before he's able to put that leg under him. He might get pneumonia or gangrene. God in heaven, I hope I'll never again have to listen to him rambling the way he was the first evening, as if he were moving in some great court with all the nobility of the world."

"Could we put him in some other house, in the house of someone we could trust?"

"Whose house?"

"Sally's maybe."

"Sally's house is right opposite Luke's, and Sally has a tongue as long as today and tomorrow. Talk sense, man. There's no house where we could put him but my house only and that's why we must tell Big John about him." She looked from one to the other of our downcast faces and said: "What is it to a ship going down? Didn't we save the man's life?"

Roddy said savagely:

"It's a pity we did. He's brought us nothing but misfortune, cross-grained old scoundrel—"

It was true that the doctor was never satisfied with his treatment, especially when he was left in Roddy's charge. They had disliked each other on sight and Roddy was not neat enough with his hands to please our elegant prisoner. He was always restless with him and kept on asking for me. For this reason I usually took trouble to keep my voice low when I came to the house, unless it was my spell of duty. This time I had forgotten, however, and sure enough my voice had penetrated to the next room.

"Pat! Pat!" I heard the doctor bellow, in a voice that he knew would bring me running.

I made a face at the others, and went into the room off the kitchen, dragging my feet, reluctant to face him. Before I had my hand on the latch, the doctor's voice came strongly from the bedroom again:

"Come in, boy, come in! What's keeping you? I know you're there. Move smartly, please!"

In a day or two I'll be moving smartly into Galway gaol, I thought, or maybe I'll be transported to Van

Diemen's Land. We had some terrible songs about the sufferings of the people in those places. Inishgillan suddenly looked small and very sweet to me. No more would I see the herring shoal riding in from the Atlantic, piloted by the frantic gulls. No more would I see the porpoises leaping and flying over a calm summer sea. No more would I see the fin of a basking shark cutting through the waves like the sail of a little boat, nor see the strong men of Inishgillan go out to capture him with their harpoons in their currachs, every man as brave as Odysseus sailing into hell in the black, black ship. Instead, I would be lying in my chains in Galway gaol, wishing that I had never laid an eye on the snarling gentleman that had landed me there.

His voice brought me to my senses when I was inside the room:

"Well? Asleep on your feet? Where have you been? That other boy is an ignoramus, a clown. His hands are like turnips and his brain is like a pot of porridge." He stopped suddenly and said in an entirely different tone: "Why do you look at me like that? Are you planning to murder me, perhaps?"

"If we were going to do that, wouldn't we have done it first instead of last?"

"I suppose so. But I don't like the look of you. I'm getting well, you know. Very soon I'll be on my feet. Then I'll walk out through that doorway, and find some sensible man on this island, and tell him how I have been treated. After that, I think we won't see much of each other—for a while."

"You won't have to wait the few days at all, I'm thinking."

"Why not?"

"Because the most sensible men on this island will very soon be coming up to have a look at you."

A moment before, I had heard Roddy's feet running past the window. I guessed that he was on his way down to summon Big John and my father, and probably Luke and one or two others, for a conference in Mamó's kitchen.

The doctor was surprised, as I could see, and he did not know what to think of this news. He had had plenty of time to reflect while he lay there in bed during the long days, and he must have realised that we were keeping his presence secret from the rest of the island. No doubt his hope of being rescued had always been in the chance that he would one day get away from our clutches and throw himself on the mercy of some kindly islander. It was terrible to see the hope of this drain away from his face, and despair settle there instead. I was not too preoccupied with fears for my own future to feel some sympathy for him, but I did not tell him that I thought his freedom was very near.

"Would you like to play a game of chess?" I said, to divert him.

He had taught me how to play this game, which was quite new to me. Among his instruments in the box that we had brought him from the ship, there had been a pocket chessboard, with tiny chessmen, each fitted with a peg that held it upright on the board. I was already a champion at draughts, and I learned the new game quickly. I had noticed that this had pleased the doctor very much, and he had been far more cheerful since we had begun to play. Also, he obviously delighted in teaching me and in explaining the moves and the strategy of the game.

He agreed to play now, and I got the board from the table by his bed. Very soon we were both moving all the nobility of the world around on the board. I told him what Mamó had said, and how she had interpreted his ramblings. It was a real pleasure to hear him laugh.

He had a great capacity for cutting himself off from his surroundings and concentrating on the game, so that he did not hear the men arrive and go into the kitchen. Perhaps he thought that the murmur of voices that came to us presently was only Mamó and Roddy having a chat. But I knew that a great discussion was going on out there, and I longed to hear it. I could not keep my mind on the game. I was beaten in half of the usual time.

"Your queen is gone," the doctor said, "and your knight is finished too, and that's my game. You must learn to see what my strategy is, not just plan your own—"

He started off on the lesson that he always gave on the game, but I could not understand a word of it today. I stood up and said:

"I'll see if your dinner is ready."

And before he had time to say he was talking of chess, and not of dinner, I was out of the room.

I shut the door quickly to keep the doctor as long as possible in ignorance of how many visitors we had. Big John was there, and Sidecar Connor and my own father. Just as I shut the bedroom door behind me, Luke Hernon and Bartley MacDonagh appeared on the doorstep and darted softly into the room. Their rawhide shoes made no sound on the stone floor. They looked quickly around at the anxious faces of Big John and Sidecar and Mamó. Then Bartley said sharply:

"What's up? Is there someone dead? Ye're like a wake."

"Ssh!" said Mamó. "He'll hear you. Come over here and sit down till we talk."

Bartley went across and sat on a creepy stool by the fire. Luke took the place on the hob that had been left for him, and said in a low voice:

"Who will hear us? What are you talking about?"

"'Tis a man off the ship," Mamó said.

Roddy and I stayed very silent, hoping that she had undertaken the unpleasant task of telling what we had done. She was just as responsible as we were, so I felt no scruples at leaving it to her.

"The two boys here found him on the strand, and he half drowned, the night of the *Coriander*," said Mamó. "They brought him here. He's within in the room for the past two weeks, in the big bed."

"Why?"

"Mending a broken leg."

"Why didn't you send him down to the slip the day Willie O'Connell came—"

Suddenly Luke stopped and gazed at Mamó as if she had two heads. Then he said wonderingly:

"He's the doctor! The doctor that the captain was lamenting about! You had him here all the time!"

Mamó nodded. Neither of us said a word. Bartley said:

"Well, that beats Banagher, and Banagher beat the devil. What kind of a man is he?"

"A cross, thin kind of a man."

"Is he healthy?"

"He is, faith, but for his broken leg, and that will be soon mended."

"And now you want to send him with the Revenue Men?" Luke asked, still puzzled by the whole situation.

"We do not, then," said Mamó. "It's the last thing we want, after all our trouble."

There was a long, long pause. There was no need for any further explanations, since the men were able to understand exactly what had happened. We could almost see the thoughts hopping around inside their heads as they considered what we had done and speculated about the future. There was no way of knowing how they would take it. Luke was so law-abiding, that was our principal trouble. He felt his position as the representative of the Government, and it gave him a feeling of responsibility for the morals of all of us. Big John, being a travelled man, felt rather the same, which was easy to understand. He had seen and done more in his life than everyone else on the island put together, and an experienced man must be listened to with respect.

Mamó must have seen some change in their expression that encouraged her. She was watching them closely enough, certainly. She said:

"We had meant to keep the doctor until after the Revenue Men would be gone. What they wouldn't know wouldn't trouble them. But when you said I should have two of them here, I knew we'd have to let you in on the secret."

"You can't have the Revenue Men here now," Luke said quickly.

"Lukeen, are you telling me you think we did right?" Mamó asked delightedly.

Luke looked a bit sheepish and said:

"I don't know. I never heard tell of the like of this. 'Tis abduction and kidnapping in the first degree. 'Tis highly dangerous and no mistake."

"That's why we're asking your advice," said Mamó sweetly.

In this way she handed over the problem of how to keep custody of the doctor to all the men.

"As long as I'm in the world, we're wanting a doctor in Inishgillan," said Sidecar. "Now he comes sailing in to us on the tide. I'm telling you this, that if you were to hand over that gift of the sea to the Revenue Men along with all the other lovely things, I'd set sail for Portland to my daughter Bridget by the next ship that would call into Galway. I'd say this island is finished. I'd say we'd never again see a good day, when God's gift would be sent away again—"

"All right, Sidecar, all right," said my father. "We're keeping the doctor. But how are we going to do it?"

"Tell me first how could he get away?" Sidecar demanded. "Sure, we can hardly get off Inishgillan ourselves, not to mind a stranger and a city man that wouldn't know a currach from a pookaun."

Luke stood up.

"We'd best have a look at him, before we decide. He'd need to be tough and hardy to stand the winter winds, and he'd need to be well covered with flesh against the cold. A weighty man wouldn't do either, for he'd have to be able to climb to the top of the island on a windy night maybe, bringing help to the sick."

"Anyone would think you were buying a bullock," said Mamó. "He is as he is. He's the best we can get. We're so long without a doctor that I'm not inclined to look and see if his teeth are good before we take him in. So long as he won't poison the sick people with the wrong medicines, that's good enough for me."

"'Tis true, indeed," said all the men.

They followed her in an awkward group to the bedroom door. No one wanted to be the first in. It was almost as if they expected that the doctor would bite, they hung back so shyly. Mamó walked into the room ahead of them and said in a strong, cheerful way:

"Here's a few fine men to visit you, Doctor. You must be getting tired of having no one to talk to but two boys and an old woman. Come in, men, come in!"

They came into the room and she introduced them one by one. We stood in the doorway, watching. The doctor was sitting up in bed wearing some beautiful blue pyjamas from his cabin on the *Coriander*. He looked as clean and fresh as a new baby, but no baby ever had the venomous glare of him. One eyebrow was raised and his jaw was thrust outwards, and his voice came like the sting of a jellyfish.

"I'm very glad to see you, indeed. And I hope there's a man among you with an ounce of decency in him that will get me off this wretched island without delay."

"Easy on, easy on, now," said Sidecar. "You'd best be getting fond of the island and leave off calling it names, for you're likely to live out the remainder of your days here. 'Tis a nice little island, as many will tell you—"

"I'll have the law on you!" said the doctor in a grating tone. "You'll be in gaol, the whole lot of you!"

"There isn't much law on this island," said Bartley. "Only what we make ourselves. And there isn't a gaol of any sort or size. Let you content yourself now, for we mean you no harm."

"No harm, you say, and you keep me here a prisoner!"

"Would you rather we had left you to drown below on the strand?" Roddy asked suddenly. "I'm thinking that was to be your fate if we hadn't come along."

"The fact that you saved my life doesn't give you the right to keep me here for ever," said the doctor, but now he sounded just a little more friendly.

Luke said hesitantly:

"We don't wish you any harm. We are not bad people. There's some that would rob you, and murder you for your money, but we're not like that. 'Tis the way with us that we need a doctor here—"

"I know. The boys told me."

"Then there's no need for me to tell you again. You won't come to any harm. We'll let you live free here on the island. All we ask is that you cure the people when they get sick, and hide yourself away whenever strangers come to the island."

"And you think I'll do that? You think that's a small thing to ask?"

"Small or big, 'tis what you must do. And now we'll say good day, for I can see there's no more use in talking to you. You can be thinking about it until I see you again."

"Who are you?"

"Luke Hernon, at your service, sir."

We all went back to the kitchen. I had half-expected that the doctor would roar and shout after us, as I should certainly have done in his position, but instead he was very quiet. This made me rather uneasy, and I looked back at him as I shut the door. His eyes were closed, and he looked as if the weight of the world was down on top of him.

Big John had been very quiet in the doctor's room. Out in the kitchen, he stood with his back to the fire and said:

"This is something I never heard the like of before. And still there's great sense to it. The people will all be delighted when they hear of it, but I'm thinking we

won't tell them yet awhile. We'll wait until the Revenue
Men are gone again, and then we'll tell them that we kept
the best thing on the *Coriander* after all."

And this was what we did. Luke's message had caused
great excitement in Galway. Within an hour the Revenue Men were on their way to Inishgillan, all dressed up
in their fine navy-blue overcoats and caps with gold
braid on them. They came on the pilot boat, which is a
good one for a rough sea, and that was what they
expected when they set out for Inishgillan. Once you get
beyond the Aran Islands, the waves get wild and heavy,
and you have to be an islander born and bred to guess
what they're going to do next. Mattie O'Brien from
Inishthorav was an islander, of course, and all the mainland men relied on him to tell them in good time if their
last hour had come. The crew of the pilot boat were
Claddagh men from Galway, good sailors in their way
but just a little like a seagull that would be short a few of
the feathers in one wing and would be wishing he didn't
have to leave the ground at all.

"Claddagh men," said Sidecar patronisingly as we
stood by the slip watching them bring the boat around
to her moorings. "They had good men there until the
Battle of Jutland. Those fellows couldn't stay at home
only out all the time after wars and adventures. There
were hundreds of them lost in that battle, so I've heard
tell, and the little children had to figure out for themselves how to sail the pookawns afterwards for they
hadn't a father between the lot of them to teach them the
skill of it. 'Twas a terrible battle, and some mighty ships
were lost, ay, and some of their goods came sailing this
way months afterwards—"

No one was listening to him by this time, because the

currachs were being launched to bring the men ashore. My father went out, and Luke, and two men from the nearest house to the slip. These were twins called Conneeley, Simon and Stephen. Because of the position of their house, they were jealous of anyone going to sea before themselves, and they always did their best to get their boat into the water first. They were very silent, with no need to speak much, it seemed, because their main interest was in each other and each of them usually seemed to know what the other was thinking of. This saved them a lot of time and trouble. They were very tall and thin and lively, and sitting on the thwarts of their currachs they seemed always about to spring up into the air, they were so full of restless energy. They got to the pilot boat just as her anchor rattled down into the sea, and in a moment they were filling up with Revenue Men. That currach took the four of them, and my father and Luke took four men of the pilot boat's crew, that would be needed to load the goods off the *Coriander*.

As the twins' currach reached the slip, Big John went down as far as it to hand the men ashore and make them welcome. Big John was a great gentleman always, and he complimented the men on their looks and on the speed with which they had come.

"And 'tis our good fortune to have some wrack to hand over to ye," he said, "for it gives us an opportunity of having a bit of good company."

"Where is the wrack?" Mattie O'Brien asked curtly.

"It's up at Luke's place. We thought it would be the most fitting—"

Mattie turned on his heel and began to stamp off up the road. The other men had better manners and they had a word or two with Big John, thanking him for his welcome, before following their colleague.

With hardly a word, the crowd of us dispersed. It was a lovely, breezy, spring day, and the time for planting the potatoes was running out. The men went off to their fields, looking a little embarrassed, as if it was they, and not Mattie, who had been guilty of such bad manners.

Roddy and I started after Luke and the others to go up to the post office. Neither of us was old enough to have complete charge of any one task, and this left us beautifully free to present ourselves helpfully wherever the most interesting work happened to be going on.

We took a short cut and reached the post office a few minutes before the procession that was coming by the road. Molly was peeping out over the half door every twenty seconds, and then running back to lift the lid of the potato pot that was hanging over the fire. It was a huge round pot, the same as we all had, holding about ten gallons. It was full to the very top with fine potatoes, and the water was gurgling and chuckling all around these in a way that would make your mouth water. The choicest potatoes were for the Christians, naturally, and when they would have finished, the hens and pigs would have the remainder.

Molly posted me at the door to watch, so that she could give all her attention to the pot. With Roddy's help, she lifted it off the crane on which it hung, and swung it out to stand on its three short legs in the middle of the floor. Then she got a piece of sacking, and half-covered the top of the pot with it, and together they drained the water off into a basin.

"I wish I had a basket," she said, " a flat basket of sally rods, that I'd pour the potatoes into. 'Twould look fine on the table in front of visitors. I wish I had a basket like that."

"I'll make you one, Molly," I said, for the longing in her voice had started an ache in my chest. "There's sallies below by the pool. I made one for my mother a month ago. It won't take me too long."

She started to call down blessings from heaven on me. I was very glad to have made such friends with her again. In an island like ours, it is a bad thing not to be good friends with everyone. I cut her short by saying:

"Here they come!"

We all set to lifting hot potatoes out of the pot onto the oilcloth-covered table, and making a little mountain of them, so that when Mattie O'Brien's sour face appeared in the doorway, their steam was already rising up to the rafters.

"Come in and ye're heartily welcome," said Molly and she placed a chair for every man of them.

She put a huge print of butter at each end of the table, and a little heap of salt at each corner and then she said:

"Now, let ye eat up heartily first and we'll talk business afterwards."

"The Lord spare you your health," said one of the Claddagh men, and he got to work on a potato.

"May you never see a poor day."

"May you not spend as much as one day sick this year."

"God strengthen your hand."

One by one they started to eat, each with some blessing on the house or on its owners, all except Mattie O'Brien. He blessed himself silently before he began to eat, it's true, and this proved that he was not an out-and-out pagan, but never a word of blessing did he say on the woman that had cooked his dinner. He filled himself with her food, though, as we all noticed. Indeed he seemed a little softer when he had finished, but perhaps that was the kindness that comes from the stomach rather than the one from the heart.

At last they all pushed back their chairs and went to look at the bales of suits that were piled up until they filled one end of the long kitchen. They tested the cloth as we had done, and praised its strength and its beauty. Mattie said then:

"'Tis a hard thing on ye to hand all that fine stuff over to the Government, I'm thinking."

"'Tis, sure," said Big John, "but we'd scruple to keep such valuable things."

"It must be a change before death," said Mattie rudely.

"Now, listen to me, young man," said Big John. "You can do your business in a civil way, same as everyone else, or I'll know where to lay my complaints."

"I'm just wondering why these suits are not wet, nor even stained with sea water. How long have ye got them here?"

"Not long."

"Not long enough for them to have dried? Nor for the stains to have disappeared by a miracle?"

"They were never wet. They came in a ship. We got them ashore before she foundered."

"Ah, yes. The *Coriander*. We heard of her. The people off that ship were brought into Galway, and they said they saw their ship sitting on the rocks by the slip one evening like a granny sitting with her knitting by the fire. The very next morning she was gone."

"How long would she sit there?" Luke demanded. "You must have felt the storm even inside in Galway."

"She wouldn't stay long there when the Inishgillan

men would be about her," said Mattie.

"'Twas ungrateful talk," said Luke, "after we saving their lives. They'd all be feeding the fishes this minute if it wasn't for the Inishgillan men."

"Ye lost one, I hear."

"They told you that?"

"Yes, the doctor, they said, the light of heaven to his soul."

"Amen," said Luke piously.

"Not a sign of him since, I suppose, though his corpse will be along one of these days, the poor man. And the ship is gone down?"

"You didn't see her on the rocks."

"No, I did not. I'd say the fairies took her only that I don't believe in fairies any more."

The rest of us were very silent during this dialogue, not knowing what might happen next. Luke put his face very close to Mattie's and said softly:

"Mister, did you come out here to inquire about the *Coriander*, or did you come out because I sent word into Galway that we saved some of her cargo? If you don't know the answer to that question I can telegraph right from this house and get it for you."

"I'm only asking questions, innocent questions," said Mattie.

"A dangerous occupation," said Luke. "Now, let you get on with the business that brought you. 'Twill take the afternoon, if I'm any judge. Then we'll have supper, and a fine drop of the hard stuff, and for the rest of the evening we'll be telling stories and making sport as all Christians do when the light of day is gone. Tomorrow morning you can start off early with your little ship and you'll be in Galway in the afternoon."

"That was my own plan," Mattie said amiably enough, and we knew from his tone that he had decided not to question us any further.

The afternoon was spent in counting and loading, and before darkness fell, the suits were all stored below decks on the pilot boat. Then, as Molly had fed the men at midday, they had their supper at our house. Big John and Luke and Sidecar came along to entertain them while they ate.

My mother had two huge new cartwheels of soda-bread for them, and plenty of butter. As I helped her to set the table with flowery mugs before the men came, she said to me:

"And I have eight eggs, one for each of them. Isn't it a queer thing that those old hens of ours wouldn't lay an egg for ourselves this week, and now the day the Revenue Men are here, they lay eight of them? 'Tis a sign from heaven, I suppose, and they'll have to get them, though I grudge them sore."

"It's the warm weather that makes them lay," I said, laughing at her, but there were tears of annoyance in her eyes as she placed an egg before every man.

We had a good evening's sport, sure enough, and the Revenue Men got more polite after they finished their work. The crew had gone back to sleep on the pilot boat when they had finished their supper, and we had only the other four to suffer. Watching them sitting there in Andy Folan's shop, in the best places by the fire, each man with a glass of fine black porter in his hand, it seemed to me that it was like seeing four dogs being entertained by a household of cats. The men of the island were so careful and discreet that you'd think to listen to us that we spent our time on the look-out for ways of helping the Government to keep down the taxes, and that we were always watching our chance to go galloping over to the mainland with baulks of timber and sacks of flour that had been washed ashore and that lay heavily on our consciences. It was true that every man there felt lighter for having given up the suits, but as the evening went on it seemed to me that they were liking the four Revenue Men less and less. Then Sidecar began to tell stories about the time of the Armada, when the Spanish soldiers came ashore in their dozens, with their fine horses.

"That's a thing you never get off a ship nowadays is a horse," said Sidecar. "And 'twould be a useful thing, as useful—"

My father nudged him into silence with his knee and got him back presently onto the old stories of Finn MacCool and the Fianna. Those people lived a thousand years before revenue was invented, so it was a safe subject. Then we heard all the news of Galway, and that the big liners would soon be calling there again on their way to America. I was very much interested in this because though I had often heard of these huge ships I had never seen one. They had not come by Galway for nearly twenty years.

"They're a wonder to see," said Sidecar. "There were liners came past here and they had a bigger population on them than this island, ay, and bigger than the biggest Aran island."

So the chat and the talk went on until it was time to go to bed. The two men who were to have been billeted with Mamó stayed in our house instead, and I slept in the kitchen. They grumbled a bit to each other about the smallness of my bed, after they had gone into the room.

I could hear them through a crack in the door that shut off my room from the kitchen. I slept uneasily, with one ear cocked lest they might come out during the night and go up to Mamó's house and find the doctor. It was an absurd fear, of course. That night I learned a great lesson which has been useful to me ever since: never to take any heed of night thoughts and fears, for they have little or nothing to do with reality.

Towards morning the wind sprang up, that had been silent for four days. It crept around the house quietly at first. Then it rolled a barrel along the ground outside, slowly but surely, as a man would push it in front of him. Then I heard it brush through the dry stalks of wallflowers that were still standing from last year against the house wall.

I got out of the settle bed and went to the door and opened it softly. Away down below me, the Killaney Light was ringed in white foam and the sea was a dull grey. I thought with admiration of Big John, how well he had forecast what would happen. The light was growing every moment and the darkness was slipping away even while I watched. Out of space, it seemed, the hillside opposite the house appeared, with quiet nibbling sheep quite unsurprised. The Killaney Light flashed once more, very white, and then it was turned off. I made a noise with shutting the half-door loud enough to waken everyone, and began to put on my clothes.

Sure enough, within a few minutes the two men appeared rubbing their eyes. Once they had peered out at the weather, they no longer looked sleepy. They began loudly asking for their breakfast and saying that they must be off.

"We're lucky if we get home," they said. "There's a

storm on the way again. Ye're never without a storm in this God-forsaken place. The tea, woman, the tea!"

"'Tis a pity ye must be off so soon," my mother said, placidly pouring the tea, "just when we were getting fond of ye."

They looked at her suspiciously. Then one said to me curtly:

"Over to the post office, boy, and tell the others to get up. We must be going at once."

But there was no need for me to move. Just then Mattie O'Brien came stumping to the door.

"If ye don't want to be here for a month, ye'd best be on the road in five minutes."

And he was gone again.

It seemed as if our two guests liked us as little as we liked them, for they wolfed the remainder of their food and ran from the house as though it were on fire, hardly pausing at the door for a moment to bid my mother good-bye and to thank her for her hospitality. Then they were off down the hill like rabbits with the dogs after them. The twins' currach was waiting to hurl them across the stretch of sea that separated the pilot boat from the slip, and a few minutes after they had climbed on board, the pilot boat went scooting away for the safety of Galway.

"Good riddance of bad rubbish," said Big John as we turned back up the hill. "Now we must pass on the good news about the doctor."

Chapter Five

That morning Big John visited every house on the island and told the people of our piece of wrack, the doctor. Not a single man but was delighted with the news, and they all agreed with Sidecar that it would never do to send him away when he had come to us from heaven.

"You can have too much of that kind of thing," they said, still sorry about the suits.

At dinner-time, Big John came up to Mamó's house to have a talk with the doctor and to give him some advice. I went with him, but Luke had seized Roddy and made him stay in to learn how to use the telegraph. That was to be Roddy's work when Luke would be too old for it. Everyone was glad of this, because the postmaster is an important man and Roddy was agreed to be a steady, reliable choice for it. No one thought of asking him whether he would like the job, but he had told me privately that he was looking forward to it, and that the knowledge that it was waiting for him made him give up all thoughts of going off to the New World to seek his fortune. You may be sure that I was glad to hear this, because it was good to know that when I would be an old man heaving myself up the hill from the slip on a stick,

Roddy would be doing the same thing a yard behind me. Somehow this took the sting out of the thought of getting old, which had nibbled at me more than once lately.

"We're moving the doctor down to your place," Big John said to me as we reached Mamó's door. "Mamó's had enough to do for him in the last while. She looks tired and a bit craw-sick. It's no joke at her age to have to listen to his grumbles as well as cook his meals and tend to his bed."

"What about my mother?"

"She'll like it fine. I asked her, and she was willing."

There was no time for any more. I guessed that there was another good reason why the doctor was to be moved. Our house was about half-way along the road to the slip, and it could be reached easily from any house on the island. I thought it was clever of Big John to have thought of this. It was nothing to some of the other things he had thought of, as I was soon to discover.

We found the doctor sitting in the kitchen in a big chair by the fire, facing towards the door. Blankets from his bed were tucked around his knees. His sharp face was the same creamy yellow as the wool of the blankets. Only his eyes moved when we came in, lifting to stare at us like two stinging flies. Mamó was sitting on the creepie stool at the opposite side of the fire, tending a loaf of bread in the pot-oven. She had a rather hunted look about her, and I guessed that she had vainly been trying to improve his humour. She welcomed us as Noah must have welcomed the dove, the day long ago when he brought the olive branch back to the ark.

"Come in, come! Sit down. Big John, 'tis fresh and well you are looking! Patcheen, you're growing up into a fine man, God bless you!"

"God save all here," said Big John, winking at me as he hung his broad black hat on the peg by the door. "I didn't know you had so much admiration for the pair of us. And how is our friend today?"

"I'm worrying about him, getting out of bed so soon."

"I've told her I know what I'm doing," the doctor said impatiently. "If I don't get up and move around, I'll have other complaints as bad as a broken leg and worse. But she won't believe me. I had to fight my way out here."

I guessed that Mamó preferred to have her kitchen to herself and that this was one reason why she had wanted him to keep to his bed. A moment later she said apologetically:

"'Tisn't but I like his company. 'Tis just that I'm afraid for his health."

"He should be a good judge of that," said Big John. "Now tell me, Doctor, how long will it be before you can walk?"

"Two or three weeks. It's mended nicely. Why do you ask?"

"We're thinking of moving you down where you'll have more company."

"Whose company?"

"The company of other people like myself. That's all we can offer you. Some of us have travelled a bit. There's none of us educated. But we do the best we can."

The doctor flushed and said:

"I had not meant to insult you."

"Good," said Big John. "Now, you know the way things are. You'll live well in the house of this boy's mother. When strangers come to the island you'll come back to this house and stay quiet until they go away again. You can stay at the back of the church on Sundays when the priest comes over from Bofin. We don't want to part you from God."

"That's very nice of you," the doctor said solemnly.

"'Tis not easy to do a thing like this."

"I have no doubt of that. Just don't expect sympathy from me."

Big John sighed.

"Maybe when you have been here for a while, you'll see that there's reason in it. Tell me now, are you any good to pull a tooth?"

"I have done it on occasion, though I'm not a dentist."

"We don't need a dentist, only an odd tooth pulled. What kind of a hand are you at surgery?"

"Just what came my way. I was a general practitioner. Do you know what that is?"

"Yes. My nephew is one, in Boston."

The doctor looked at him as if he had said his nephew was a wild animal. There was a long silence. Then Big John said kindly:

"My nephew was always a great scholar. He'd be my brother's son, the brother that was younger than myself. He went off to Boston to the uncle, that's my other brother that's out there for years, and he worked for a while there, and saved his money, and went to medical school, and that's how it happened," Big John said, as if he were apologising for it.

The doctor was glaring in his most terrifying way.

"And why doesn't he come back and practise medicine on this benighted island?"

"Sure, there's no money to be made here. It's different for you. You have your fortune made, or you wouldn't be going sailing around the world on the *Coriander* as the sailors told me. And you have neither wife nor child. My nephew has a big family over there in Boston, all going to schools and colleges. What would they say to him if he told them he was lighting out for an island off the coast of Ireland, and that they would have to come along with him? When they're all finished and done for, he'll maybe come home, like many another, but we must be fair to him. He'll send over any drugs you want. I'm sure of that, though I didn't ask him."

"It's all arranged," the doctor said in a wondering tone.

"Not everything. There will be many a thing I haven't thought of that you can put me right on. The main thing is that you won't want for drugs. And I'd like to give you a piece of advice."

"To keep my temper! To keep my temper! For fear I might break a blood-vessel!"

"Ah, now, Doctor! There's no need to be angry. Don't upset yourself, or you won't be in the better of it."

"No. I should sit here smiling like a baby, I suppose."

"Be reasonable, Doctor. You wanted to see the world. Isn't it all one to you what part of it you see?"

"That doesn't sound reasonable to me."

"So you should learn patience," said Big John as if the doctor had not spoken, "and don't be all the time telling the people you don't want to be here. If you do that, they won't like it."

The doctor fell silent at this, and he did not speak again as long as Big John stayed in the house. I had been amazed at what I had heard, Big John pretending to be a bit foolish, as if he did not understand why the doctor did not want to stay with us. And still there must have been wisdom in what he had done, since it had silenced the doctor's grumbles. Big John's last remark had sounded like a threat. I wondered how long it would work.

When Mamó's loaf was baked, she made tea for us. Still the doctor never spoke, as long as big John remained in the house. He took his tea from Mamó and drank it silently, gazing into the fire, as if he had a lot to think about. I noticed that she had given him one of her very best china cups, and that he had a saucer with it. These cups and saucers were the finest that money could buy in Galway. They were white with a gold rim and handle, and roses that were so wonderfully drawn that you could almost smell the scent of them. Big John and Mamó and I had great big mugs, with flowers too, but it seemed fitting that the doctor should have something more delicate. I resolved to warn my mother that she should get out her best things for him, and then it occurred to me that she would probably think of this herself.

She did think of it. Later that evening, my father and Big John together borrowed the best horse and cart on the island for the task of transporting the doctor to our house. It was a fine cart with springs and it belonged to Andy Folan of the shop, who was my father's cousin. As well as having the shop, Andy was a blacksmith by trade. He was very skilled, and he could make fine gates and railings when he had the materials and the mind to use them. This did not happen very often, because the shop took up a great deal of his time. Besides, he was a sociable man, and he often spent long hours in chat and conversation and discoursing when he could have been working in the forge.

Not only did the cart have springs but it also had rubber tyres on its wheels instead of a metal rim. Any island man could tell at once that it was a shopkeeper's cart, because it was too delicate for the kind of hard wear that our carts endured. They had to clank and grind over rocks and stones and sand, and sometimes down into the sea when we were cutting weed off the rocks at low tide. Andy's cart sailed along with a whirring sound that made Sidecar shake his head with longing for his namesake. It was used mainly for carrying goods from the slip to the shop.

I felt quite proud of it when it arrived at Mamó's door to take the doctor down to our house. The tall white pony was quiet. Between them, Big John and Luke carried the doctor in his chair out to the roadway. Then they lifted him like a baby onto the cart and drove very gently down the hill, as if it were a sitting hen and a clutch of eggs that they had up there. Everyone came out to the doors to see the doctor go by. Following the cart, I knew that the people were all longing to run out of their houses and have a good look at him and say a few words of welcome. But they were afraid that their curiosity would be impolite and so they restrained themselves. I was glad of this, for it was clear that he found the little journey painful. When the cart stopped at our door he looked almost as he had done on the day when we had first found him.

We got him into the house somehow, and into my bed. I was scarcely able to recognise my own room when I saw it. The curtains that my sister had sent from Portland were hanging at the window. The embroidered sheets and bedspread were on the bed and a clean cloth, that I had never seen before, was on the table beside it. There was a lustre jug on the mantel with a handful of early spring flowers and leaves of grass. All these with the whitewashed walls made the little room look like a palace for a king.

We stood and watched him for a moment, waiting, I suppose, for a kind word about the room. The doctor said not a word and presently we went out to the kitchen in silence.

In a moment old Mamó came trotting in, out of breath.

"How is he? How did he manage the journey?"

"Fine," my father said. "He's tired, of course. We must expect that."

By his uneasy look I knew that he was thinking it was not going to be very pleasant to have this cranky stranger for ever blighting our happy house.

"He was quiet with me at first," Mamó said. "After a while he softened out a bit. He likes a drop of good soup, and he likes a few lamb chops— not one, mind you, but three or maybe four. He likes his tea strong and his egg soft. He doesn't like the bacon boiled with the cabbage only boiled by itself in a little pot. A queer idea, but why wouldn't he have it the way he likes it? Put a few handfuls of brown flour in the cake of bread, and when you make white bread, put sultanas in it. He loves the sultana bread."

In the very same way I have heard women give instructions for the care of a pup or a kitten that they had reared from birth. Mamó went to the bedroom door.

"I'll go in and have a word with him."

She opened the door and went in. After a sign from my father, my mother reluctantly followed her, leaving the door open, so that we could hear what Mamó was saying:

"There you are, as snug as a bug in a rug, Doctor!

When the fine days will be here, let you take a chair outside the door. No, two chairs you'll need. Put your leg up on one and put your bo-hind on the other—excuse my language! Herself here will help you with the chairs, for she has a good heart and you won't meet a nicer woman on the whole island."

Suppressing their chuckles, the men moved nearer to the door to hear better. Then the doctor's voice came, soft and clear and full of kindness:

"Thank you, Mamó. I'll take your advice about the chairs. And I'm sure that myself and Mrs Folan will get on well together."

We looked at each other in astonishment at his gentleness, while Mamó's voice went on:

"That's right, Doctor. And I'll be in to see you every day of the week and sometimes twice, and when you're able to walk again we'll have great times with céilí and singing all the summer long. So get yourself well as quickly as you can."

"I'll do that, Mamó," said the doctor in the same gentle voice.

"If that doesn't beat all!" said Big John very softly. "He's settled down. Thanks be to God!"

"Amen," said my father doubtfully. "I don't want to be a gaoler. I hope he'll be happy in himself. But how can he be happy when he'd rather be away from us?"

"Horses don't like work, either," Big John said, "but they do it just the same."

"You can't compare a man with a horse. 'Twouldn't be Christian."

"Are you changing your mind about him? Do you want to let him go?"

"No. I don't want that. I know we need him sorely. I

just want for him to be a bit at ease."

"We'll see how it goes," said Big John and he went off without going into the bedroom again.

It was true that my mother was renowned for her kindness. She followed Mamó's directions about the food as carefully as if she had written them down that first evening and studied them for a week. When my father suggested that she was burdened too heavily with the extra work, she silenced him with talk of charity.

"And he's a good polite gentleman," she said. "I never once heard him say a harsh word, only always thanking me and telling me there is no need to take so much trouble for him."

It was true that he was like this with my mother and with Mamó when she came to visit him. But with myself and with the men he was like a conger eel. He would fix a flat eye on us, full of dislike, and his voice would be kept low and rasping so that the women could not hear it.

"Thieves! Kidnappers! Scoundrels! Every man of you will be in gaol yet for this. If your arms and legs were to fall off, I wouldn't lift a finger to help you. You can do your own doctoring as you always did, before ever I had the misfortune to be washed up here. It was a pity I wasn't drowned that night of the *Coriander's* wreck." And worst of all: "I was with the *Coriander* in the South Seas, where they say there are cannibals living still, that would make a meal of you if they got you into their clutches. Are you any better on this island? I don't think so. You're just a different kind of cannibal, that's all."

Big John looked hurt and said:

"Ah, now, Doctor! Don't say those things at all. Sure, we'd never think of—doing the like of that." He could not bring himself to be more exact. "And aren't you well cared for? Aren't you putting on flesh day by day? Isn't the good healthy colour coming back to you? You look twice the man you were when first we saw you."

"That's the kind of talk the cannibals would have too."

Big John flushed with anger.

"We don't like to have those things said of us," he said sharply.

"And I don't like to be here a prisoner."

So it went on, until the men almost gave up coming to visit him. Luke came every day and asked my mother loudly, in the kitchen, how the doctor was doing. Big John would put his head into the room every second day and look at him, but he avoided conversation. It was the same with my father and the rest of them: their consciences were troubling them a good deal, I suppose, and they felt the doctor's accusations all the more keenly for that.

He missed their visits, without a doubt. He became a regular demon for chess, calling for me at all hours to go and play with him and snorting with contempt whenever he won a game, which was very often. He drove me to improve beyond what I would ever have believed, so that I was able to beat him occasionally. When this happened he was seized with several different emotions: pride in his achievement of having taught me so well, anger at having lost the game and fear lest I might soon become as good a player as himself. He always said:

"Twenty years to make a chess player! Twenty years!"

I hoped that my mother would rescue me from this, but she would not, though there was plenty of work waiting for me in the fields with my father.

"You're doing a good work where you are," she said.

"People are more important than fields, so I've always believed. Keeping him happy is a charity, when he can't walk."

It was all the more annoying to be confined by the doctor's bed or by his chair in the kitchen when I learned from Roddy one day that the men were holding conferences about the loss of the sheep from the Grazing Island. The time was drawing near when the spring lambs should be shipped over for a few months on the good grass. Naturally no one wanted to send his sheep there, and still there was not enough grass on Inishgillan for them.

"'Tis like sending soldiers to the Crimea," said Bartley MacDonagh to my father one evening in our house. "There isn't a man on the island can afford to give a present of lambs to the fairies, or whoever is taking them."

My father had not been at the last meeting because he had been schooling a young horse to make him fit to go on the Aran Island steamer the next time she would call. He asked Bartley:

"What do they think is happening to them?"

"Some says one thing and some says another. Sidecar thinks that maybe they have found a passage into a hole of some kind and that if we could find that hole, we would find all the sheep inside it dead of starvation."

"'Tis a possibility, sure enough. If some went into a hole like that, the next would follow and the next, one after the other until they would all be within."

"Tomás Rua says they're going over the cliff. He has no doubt of it. He says they're washed away by the tide and that's why we don't find them below. Tell me now, Martin," said Bartley, "would you say that if one sheep fell over the cliff, the others would jump after her?"

"I never heard of such a thing happening," said my father, "though I'd believe anything of sheep. They're the most foolish animals that God ever made and that's the truth. If 'twas horses we had on the Grazing Island, they'd mind themselves better."

"If 'twas horses!"

They looked at each other in consternation at the very idea. We breed fine horses on our island. Though it's a cold, windy place for such delicate animals, something in the air of the island seems to suit them. Horses are worth so much that if a man were to lose one, he would lose his life too, without a doubt.

"Was any decision taken?"

"There were several suggestions, but they haven't come to a decision yet. Indeed Big John said it wouldn't be fitting to decide on anything until yourself would be there and a few others that were missing the last time."

Bartley and my father avoided each other's eyes. After a pause my father said:

"I know what they're thinking, sure enough. I suppose it will come to that."

"It must, man, it must."

"We can't afford to let them go."

My father turned to me and said heartily:

"Pat, go in there to the room and see does the doctor want for anything."

Dragging my feet, I did as I was told. I would have given a great deal to have heard the rest of the conversation. I glanced back as I shut the door and saw my father lean in eagerly and take a coal out of the fire with the tongs, to redden his pipe. I guessed that they were going to talk of the reasons why no one had yet stayed with the sheep on the Grazing Island, and why they became so solemn when it seemed that the only solution would be for someone to do this. I had heard these things spoken of on one or two occasions when I had got into a dark corner of someone's kitchen and had sat there very silent and unnoticed. The men avoided speaking of them in front of children and young people for several reasons: for fear of frightening them, and because they felt a little ashamed of believing the stories, and because the priest didn't like it.

It was not for nothing, they said, that there was no saint's name on that island. No saint would live there because every night his prayers and penances would be disturbed and interfered with by the carousing of the fairies. Since the whole of Ireland became a Christian country, it was said, the fairies had had to move out to the islands. Some had gone into the mountains and dark valleys, and they would only come out on moonlight nights to plague the decent people on their way home from a late party. I had often heard stories of a man forced to join in a game of hurley between two rival factions of fairies, who would vanish suddenly at last and leave him sitting cold in the ditch, with nothing but his aching bones to prove that he had not been dreaming. Indeed if that was all he had he would be lucky: there were stories also of men who had finished the game with their heads for ever turned back to front, or with two noses or three ears to carry through life. These would be the ones who had failed in some way to please the fairies, and their fate made everyone else mighty careful to talk civilly of the good people, even in broad daylight.

Did we believe those old stories? I don't think so. Roddy and I had had many a good laugh over the simplicity of our elders. And yet we would not have neglected to leave out a saucer of milk for the fairies on the night of Samhain, nor would we have dug the sod in a fort field for fear of offending them. Even if we did not altogether believe in them, some of the stories were hard to explain away. We kept very quiet about what we believed, because we knew that it is always well to be on the safe side in that sort of doubtful case.

I was curious to know exactly what were the stories about the Grazing Island. I had only picked up bits and pieces of them, because of being hooshed away as soon as the interesting part of the conversation began. There was talk of a man who had once brought young cattle there, and who had sat late at night by the turf fire he had made in front of the bothán where he intended to sleep. He had a pot of mangolds and turnips boiling on the fire for the cattle, and he was waiting for them to be cooked before lying down for the night.

The next thing, out of the dusk came a big ginger cat and said:

"Good evening."

"Good evening to you," said the man and he shivered with fright, knowing well that there wasn't a house on the island to keep a cat, big or small, and that this must be an unnatural one. The cat sat by the fire and said no more, only warmed himself comfortably. After a while there came a black cat and said the same to the man, and got the same reply, and sat there warming himself. After him came a tabby cat, and so on until there were twenty cats of all colours and denominations sitting by that man's fire and he nearly fainting with the fear of their flashing eyes and fierce long teeth.

When they could tell by the smell that the mangolds

were cooked, one of the cats leaned forward and took the lid off the pot and scooped out a piece from the boiling water and ate it. It should have burned the daylights out of him, but he just crunched his way through it as if it were a slice of bread. The other cats began to do the same but the man waited for no more. He gave a yell that was heard over on Inishgillan, and ran for his life down to his currach and rowed home, and frightened the life out of his wife by staggering into the kitchen at four o'clock in the morning. The cats never stirred, he said. When he was leaving the island he looked back and saw them still sitting in a ring around his fire, raiding his pot of mangolds every now and then as the fancy took them.

There were other stories, of men who had seen fairies and pookas dancing madly on the grass by the shore, sometimes with the sheep joining in, and there was a story of a man who had gone away with the fairies and was never seen again.

"He was probably drowned," Roddy said when we discussed it. "They didn't want to believe that a man could be drowned so easily so they made out that it was the fairies that took him."

"Would you spend a night there alone?" I asked.

"Not for Ireland free. But I'd go if I had someone with me. That would be different."

We had often planned how we would go out there together some night and make a big turf fire at the door of the bothán, and sit there before it waiting for whatever would come. We would bring a pot of potatoes and roast them in the ashes and feast on them until the dawn. The bothán was made of sods, with a roof of thatch. We would sleep there at last when the fire would die down and we would wake to find no one but the larks and ourselves in full possession of the island. The trouble was that our parents would never have agreed to it. We knew this so well that we did not ask them. We did not believe that there was the smallest danger in the plan, but our knowledge of the stories gave us a wonderful shiver of excitement.

That evening, when I left my father and Bartley talking, I found the doctor sitting up very straight in bed, looking even more ferocious than usual. I thought he would direct me to the chess-board immediately, but instead he said sharply:

"I hear voices in the kitchen. Who is there?"

"My father and Bartley."

"Why don't they come in here?"

"They're talking business."

"What business could they talk of in a place like this?"

"Business that's important to themselves, anyway."

"No one comes to see me now," said the doctor fretfully. "I sit in the kitchen and people look in and see me there, and then they go away again. I sit outside on a chair and everyone passing by gets suddenly interested in the sheep on the hill. They just turn their heads away and walk past. What is the matter with them?"

"They're shy of you, of course," I said, "and they know you don't want to be here—"

"Mamó was never shy of me, and she hasn't been near me for three days. I've gone over every word I said to her the last time she was here, and I can't make out how I could have offended her."

I was really sorry for him, he looked so depressed. Up to this moment it had never occurred to me that he might be lonely. My mother looked after him very carefully, taking great trouble to make sure that he had everything just as he liked it, but she was so anxious about this that she never stopped to chat with him: she was always running off to find some new comfort for him. Mamó was different. She was full of jokes and chat and gossip, and we had all noticed that the doctor looked much brighter after she had been visiting him. But none of us had noticed that she had not been in our house for three days.

"I'll run up and see her," I said, suddenly uneasy.

"Don't trouble yourself. When she wants to come, she'll come."

"She would be here long ago, if she were able," I said.

I paused just long enough to see that he had understood me, before leaving the room. My father glanced up in surprise as I ran through the kitchen, but I was gone so quickly that he had no time to stop me. It was a night of hard frost when I got out onto the road. There was a moon, and high, flying clouds. My bare feet made the stones ring and rattle. I ran every step of the way, my fears sending tingles down into my toes. Going so fast against the hill put me out of breath. When I caught sight of a faint light behind the window blind in Mamó's house, I stopped, very much relieved, to recover myself. Standing there filling my lungs with the sharp, cold air I realised after a moment that the light was not in the kitchen but in the room beside it. This was Mamó's bedroom.

I continued on my way more slowly, not at all eager now to discover what I had nearly burst my lungs for a few minutes before. When I reached the house, I found that the long door was open, though the half-door was almost fully closed. The blackness above the half-door shocked me. I peered inside, and saw the tiny flame of the Sacred Heart lamp on its bracket by the fireplace. There was no light on the hearth, not even a soft glow that would have showed that the fire had only lately died down.

I pushed the half-door open, and started back in fright as several squawking hens fluttered around me, terrified. They had been quick to find out that the usual barriers against roosting in the kitchen were down, and they had made their own of the place, as I soon discovered. Several of them were squatting on the table, more were on the settle and one or two had sat like grannies on either hob. I shot them all outside, and closed both doors after them. Then I lifted down the little lamp. By its lightness I knew it was almost dry and in any case its flame was too small to be useful.

Now that the kitchen was quiet, suddenly I could hear heavy breathing from Mamó's room. Wasting no more time, I went to the door and opened it.

The candle stood on the table by her bed. It was burned almost down to the socket, and its flame had grown tall and broad as often happens at the end of a candle's life. I held it high so that its light fell on Mamó's face as she lay on her back in bed. Her eyes were closed, and they did not flutter when they felt the light, as they would have done if she had been sleeping. The long, rasping breaths that she took were painful to hear, and her mouth was screwed up as if she were in pain. Still I could tell at a glance that she was not conscious. Her face had a bluish colour, very frightening to see. While I stood there watching, her fingers clutched at the quilt and she moaned a little to herself and rolled her head slightly on the pillow.

I waited for no more. Though she was unconscious, I

could not bear to leave her in complete darkness. I searched for candles and found them in the corner press. I lit one from the stump of the old one and stuck it upright in the soft wax. Then I went out very quietly, shutting the door after me.

If I had run fast up the hill, I flew down it. I went so fast that my head seemed always a yard in front of my feet and it was a miracle that I did not trip over my toes and break my nose before I reached my own house. My father and Bartley looked at me in astonishment. It seemed to me that they had not moved since I left them twenty minutes ago. My father said sharply:

"Something has happened. What is it?"

"The doctor," I said, and my voice was hoarse and faint. "Quickly, the doctor. He must go to Mamó's, at once, before it's too late."

Chapter Six

My father was on his feet in a moment.

"Inside, and tell him all about it."

Bartley followed us. The doctor looked up with his usual snarl when he heard the door open, but his expression changed when he saw us.

"Well? Well? What is it?"

"I don't know," I said. "Mamó is lying there, a queer blue colour. She must have been there for hours. The hens were all in the kitchen. But she had a candle, so she may have wakened up enough to light it and then collapsed again."

"Good boy," said the doctor softly. "That's an intelligent observation. What else did you see?"

I hardly recognised his tone, it was so gentle and encouraging.

"Her hands, how she clutched at the bedclothes. Please, can you come? You said you would let us all die. You said you wouldn't lift a finger to save one of us—"

"What nonsense are you talking? Of course I'll come. I have no choice. Come over here and help me. My clothes first. Then the box with my things in it—"

All three of us helped him into his clothes, a painful

business for him still. That evening he did not complain, though he usually dressed to yells and oaths that made my mother, at her work in the kitchen, bless herself and pray for his salvation. Before he had finished, Bartley said:

"I'll go for Andy's cart. I'll have it here in two shakes."

He had it at the door by the time the doctor had sorted what he thought he would need from his box. My mother came with Bartley on the cart. She had been at Andy's shop when Bartley came in, and she had heard his whispered conversation with Andy about the reason why the cart was needed.

We were a party of five, therefore, going up to Mamó's house, my mother and the doctor on the cart, myself running behind them keeping pace with the pony, and my father and Bartley following more slowly.

At the house, my mother got the fire going in no time at all, and hung a kettle of water on the crane. Meanwhile the doctor took me with him into the bedroom.

"And make sure that no one follows us," he instructed my mother. "Doctors hate to have spectators while they work."

This was my very first lesson in the practice of medicine. I remember every moment of it, and will probably remember it until the day I die. I did not realise at first that he was teaching me, until he said to me sharply:

"Never waste your energy on sympathy for the patient. There will be time enough for that when you have done something practical for her. Now, attend to me please."

I dried my tears on the sleeve of my jersey and attended to him. Through every stage of his examination he explained what he was doing.

"Always begin with a clear mind," he said. "Get rid of all preconceived ideas and start afresh. Never come to a patient expecting to find a certain disease or you'll find that disease and no other."

That evening he made me fix his stethoscope in my ears and I heard for the first time the strange grating rub of air trying to force its way into inflamed lungs.

"But that's no good if you don't know the sound of healthy lungs," he said with a return of his habitual weaselly tone. "We'll get on to that later, at home."

Mamó had pneumonia, he said, and he had various drugs in his bag which might or might not cure her.

"With a woman of her years you never can tell what will happen," he said, calmly lecturing me still while he searched through his boxes of pills for the ones he wanted.

It took great self-control on my part not to rush out of the room, wailing that it was wicked to speak of Mamó as if she were a person of no importance, a person that it would not matter whether she lived or died. I said not a word, however, and I was rewarded with an approving eye cocked at me as we left the bedroom together.

That was the beginning of the doctor's work on Inishgillan. Mamó could not be left alone for the first days, and he stayed right there in the house with her until she made her first progress on the road to recovery.

During those days, he instructed the neighbour women in the art of nursing. Every one of them owned one or two white aprons, which were being carefully preserved to wear when the priest came for the stations. This was when Mass was said in someone's house, and the woman of the house gave breakfast afterwards to the priest and to all the congregation, numbering about twenty, consisting of the people from the few houses nearest her. The honour of this went to every house in turn, and no woman knew when her turn would come. This was why the aprons were always ready. The doctor made them open up their clothes chests and take them out, and he said they must always wear them in the sick-room.

"Why?" Old Sally asked. "'Tisn't as if 'twas a party. Wouldn't the old blue and white checked ones do just as well?"

"You'll wear the white ones so that I can see if they are clean," said the doctor, fixing his eye on Sally.

She snorted at him a couple of times, but I noticed that she slipped out of the house and went home for her aprons at the first opportunity.

The women were in transports of admiration at the doctor's skill as a nurse. They could hardly understand how a man could take such trouble, how gentle and efficient he was and how he thought of so many ways for making the old woman comfortable in bed. When they congratulated him, he said quite rudely:

"These are only things your common sense should tell you. Surely you know most of them already, from nursing each other when you were sick."

"No, then. We did not know them," said Luke's wife Molly, who was the quickest to learn. "And we're heartily thankful to you for teaching us these things."

The doctor seemed to profit from this lesson in good manners, and he was a little more civil afterwards.

No one complained of his rudeness.

"Sure don't we know he doesn't like an inch of ourselves, nor our island?" they said. "'Tis no wonder he's cross, the creature, and he always longing to get away."

And they took to appearing at our door with little presents for him: a pat of butter in a cabbage leaf, three brown eggs, a little sultana cake—even sometimes a bunch of wallflowers or primroses. I think these things pleased him, though he gave no sign of it and he never thanked the people who brought them.

It was the evening of the next day before Mamó opened her eyes and looked about her, and saw the doctor sitting in his usual chair at the foot of her bed. She said nothing for a long time, but we could see her looking around the tidy room, observing that the clean bedspread was not her own, then looking down at her arms and seeing that she was wearing her best nightgown. She kept her eyes on this for a few minutes and then she said, very faintly:

"Who changed my nightdress for me?"

"I did," the doctor said gently.

She blushed and put up her hands to cover her face. The doctor said:

"I wouldn't trust anyone else to do it."

She put her hands down and looked at him with a little trace of the usual sparkle in her eye.

"I'm thankful to you," she said, "and sure, what I didn't know didn't trouble me."

Then she closed her eyes again as if even that little amount of talk had wearied her. I started towards her in fright, but the doctor held me back.

"She'll sleep now," he said. "Look: her colour is different, her breathing is different. Listen to it."

"With the stethoscope?"

"No, no. There's no need to bother her with that. Later on when she is rested."

She improved slowly from that day onwards and a

great load was lifted from my heart. It was then I became convinced that the doctor's profession is one of the greatest in the whole world. Without our doctor, we might have lost in old Mamó one who had the stored wisdom and charity of years, whose company would be sorely missed in every house on the island.

After so many days of anxiety, I was glad to meet Roddy one morning, on his way down to the strand with his donkey and cart. He stopped to ask after Mamó. I said:

"She's better, thanks and glory be to God. Only for the doctor, she'd be in her grave by this time."

"'Twas a trial of him," Roddy said sourly.

He could not forget the grumbles and complaints we had endured during the first days of the doctor's stay with Mamó. I said a few words of praise for him, of his kindness and skill. Roddy interrupted me:

"Why wouldn't he do it? Isn't it his job? Life is hard for all of us and we don't lie around grousing and complaining like that old rasper."

"Was there anything on the radio about the *Coriander*?" I asked quickly, to divert him. "I haven't been down to Luke's to hear it these last few days."

"There was a piece last night, saying she was lost, and who her owners were. And it said that the Inishgillan people had saved a lot of her cargo and sent it into Galway with the Revenue Men. Sidecar was lepping mad. He was all the time hoping that the Revenue Men had been wrecked on their way into Galway that morning. Then the cargo would have come sailing back to us, all the lovely suits, and this time we'd have better sense than to send them away again."

"Sidecar would be a wrecker if he weren't such a good Christian."

"He's been thinking of it, Christian or no," said Roddy. "These last evenings below in Andy's, he's been asking Tomás Rua to tell stories about his grandfather that was said to be a wrecker. Tomás doesn't like it, and he's all the time trying to shut Sidecar up, but 'tis like trying to stop the tide. Big John has grey hairs from trying to keep the peace between them."

"And did Luke get any messages?"

This was an important question. As the only representative of the Government on the island, Luke often got messages which revealed what the officials were thinking. The knowledge we gained from them often turned in very usefully. He had got messages now, Roddy said. He was to look out for the body of the doctor, and to ask any man that would be going fishing to keep his eyes open, because it might turn up any day, with the way the seas were going. There was a description of the doctor, and a little history of him which was very interesting.

"They said he's a Clareman," Roddy said," and that means he surely won't wither away when the salty winds strike him, for the spray blows over one half of Clare County, as everybody knows. They say he retired seven or eight years ago and went to South America, finding out about the queer diseases they do be having in those places, when it would have been fitter for him to have been here on Inishgillan saving the lives of his own race and nation."

"They didn't say that!"

"No, but I'm saying it. They said he married a South American woman but that she's dead this two years—"

"Thank God for that! God rest her soul," I added quickly, for I had no wish to be haunted by a furious South American woman.

"Amen," said Roddy. "They said he was coming back to end his days in Ireland, and sure, hasn't he got his wish? Inishgillan is as much part of Ireland as Galway or Dublin or Belfast. If it weren't, why would they let us vote in the elections and pay rates and taxes?"

It was no use arguing with Roddy when he got into this kind of mood. I let it go and asked if Luke thought that everyone believed the *Coriander* to be a total wreck.

"He's not so sure. There may be inspectors out looking for her remains, he says, so they're going to try sinking the ship in the next few days, what's left of her."

I spent that morning looking at the wreck of the *Coriander* where she lay by Trá Fhada. After the Revenue Men had left, the storm that had blown them home had finished off the ship for good and all. There she lay, hove-to for the last time, her poor hull lying half-in and half-out of the high tide, the waves washing in through the vast gash that had been made in her when she had struck the Three Rocks. She looked tired and dispirited, as well she might, for she was nothing now but a hollow shell. Every part that the hand of man could unscrew or saw off had been taken out of her, so that our caves were stocked with enough fittings and furnishings to build a skyscraper. Why should we have scruples about this? Far better for us to have those things than to have them buried in the salt sea. That is what would have happened if the ship had been allowed to sail free and helpless. Not only that: she would have been a hazard to shipping as well, for no one would know where she was sunk when her last end would come. This the men of Inishgillan could not have on their consciences, and they intended to make sure that the *Coriander's* sunken bones would not cause another wreck, perhaps many years hence.

It took several days for the men to carry out their plan. They had made rollers out of some of the ship's cargo of mahogany. There was not much of this. It was all in pieces of the right height to make the mast of a pookaun, but much thicker. There was great speculation as to the possibility of building a pookaun now that all the fine timber had arrived for it. Some of the men were for risking it but they listened with respect to those who said that our seas were too rough and that the risk would be too great. Big John was against it and his word carried great weight. Tomás Rua was the chief of those who wanted to try it.

"We could be very careful about taking it out," he said. "We need only use it in the summer. 'Twould be a fine thing to be able to go into Galway to a fair, or over to Bofin or Aran for a wedding, and not be handing over a sorrowful pound for every man's passage in the steamer."

"That would be fine, indeed," said Sidecar.

"The steamer gives value for your pound," said Big John, "when it brings you back alive. Anyway, we don't know will we have the timber. We mightn't be able to rescue the rollers again after we've used them."

"'Tis true for you," said Tomás.

I could see by the light in their eyes that we were going to have great arguments and discussions about the pookaun. I was very pleased at this, for it would be a change from the eternal talk of the sheep, talk that stopped dead when any stranger was present.

A calm day and a high tide were necessary before the *Coriander* could be moved, Big John said. The high spring tides were due, and the weather favoured us within a few days. It was a gift from heaven. Early one morning, every able-bodied man on the island assembled on the strand.

Big John directed the whole affair, which could never have been achieved if the ship had not happened to be lying on the side where there was no hole. As the tide rose yard by yard, rollers were slipped under her from the sea side, so that at last the part that had been beached rose off the sand. I watched this with the other boys, for we were not allowed to take any part in it. Slipping in the rollers was a dangerous business, where one might easily have a hand taken off by the ship as it fell back. When it came to the time for the men with the currachs to start hauling her out to sea on the rollers, Big John came over to me. He was panting and hoarse, for he had been shouting instructions for hours, running here, there and everywhere and flapping his arms until he looked like a mad seagull. He lowered his voice as he took me by the shoulder and spoke into my ear:

"Pat, where is the doctor?"

"He was sitting with Mamó, the last I saw of him."

"'Twould be a fright to God if he were to come down here for a stroll, and see the ship being towed off the strand and sunk. A sight like that might burst a man's heart, Pat."

"What do you want me to do?"

"To go up and stay with him. The *Coriander* is the last lifeline that he has. 'Twould be terrible if he were to see her go down bubbling into the sea."

"I'll go," I said, and I turned away at once.

One part of me longed to see how the men would finish off the ship. Already they were gathered like a school of porpoises, sitting in their currachs, out beyond her stern, preparing to haul her away as they often hauled the huge body of a harpooned shark. It was one of the most exciting things that had ever happened on

Inishgillan, and yet another part of me did not want to see it. Already I could imagine how a thing like that would get between a man and his sleep, long, long years after it had happened. It would be like seeing murder done. I was certain that I did not want the doctor to see it either.

I was just in time. A hundred yards from Mamó's door, where the shoulder of the hill still cut off the views of Trá Fhada, I met the doctor strolling towards me. He was able to walk now, though painfully, and he limped a good deal. I stopped him to ask:

"How is she now?"

"Sitting up in bed, giving out guff." He laughed. "I've just been telling her that she'll be ready for a day's work any moment."

"I was going to walk up to the cliff," I said. "Would you like to come with me?"

He turned without a word and fell into step beside me. We went up to the very top of the cliff and stood there for a long time looking out over the great Atlantic Ocean. I hardly knew what to say to him, for I was thinking of the same thing all the time: that I had heard him laugh. It was many weeks since I had heard that sound. It was not very sweet, indeed. It was the sound you might expect to hear if a conger eel laughed, or a cross old sheepdog that would be past his work and that would amuse himself in the long hours with darting out and nipping at the small boys' bare legs as they passed. But it was the best he could do, and it surely meant that he was feeling a little more satisfied with life. I need hardly say that I dared not ask him how he felt, for I would not have drawn his complaints on me for Ireland free. His face had settled into its usual grim expression, not at all inviting.

In desperation I wondered how I would keep him occupied until the business of the *Coriander* would be finished.

"Did you know we have a weaver on Inishgillan?" I asked him suddenly.

"I'm not very much interested—" he began, and then he stopped and said, quite politely: "No. I didn't know you had a weaver. Where does he live?"

"I'll take you there."

Manus Griffin was the weaver. His house was one of a group of three, twenty yards off the road. When I was a small boy, that twenty yards seemed a great distance to me, and it was always with a sense of adventure that I would set out to visit the weaver. The three houses were placed on three sides of a square, and in the middle there was a pond from which flowed a wide smooth stream. The ducks of the houses splashed all day in the pond, wagging their silly little tails and quacking to each other in their flat voices that sounded so human at times. All around the pond, some long-ago person had built a high grassy walk, paved in the middle with a line of flat stones. When we reached the beginning of this walk, the doctor stopped to gaze at the little scene. The pond was blue, reflecting the blue sky, and the ducks were burnished bronze, with a green-headed drake darting about among them. The rushes were fresh and green with the spring sap in them. The houses had lately been whitewashed and their doors painted a brilliant red.

"It's beautiful," the doctor said, as if to himself.

Manus's house was the middle one, and beside it was the long thatched shed in which he had his loom. It was dim in there after the sunlight, and I would hardly have known he was there at all, if it had not been for the regular beat of the shuttle as he worked at the loom. It stopped in a moment, when he saw us, and he came forward slowly. He was over eighty years of age at that time and though he was thin and straight as all weavers are, he could not move very fast.

"You're the doctor," he said, with his hand out in welcome. "I was hoping you would come and visit me. We'll step into the house and Nora will make us some tea."

Nora was his daughter. She was a grandmother herself, and a widow, and she brought us into the kitchen and cut soda bread and butter for us while the kettle boiled. Then she gave me her son's latest letter from Boston to read aloud to her. Though she was not yet sixty, her sight was failing and I often did her this service. So did everyone else who came over to the house. She liked to hear the letters read many times over, but out of consideration for her neighbours, she never asked the same person to read a letter twice. Also, out of politeness, she kept up a little game of pretending that she had never heard the letter before, giving little exclamations at each bit of his news.

In the meantime, Manus and the doctor talked to each other. Within five minutes they seemed like lifelong friends. Manus began by thanking the doctor for his kindness to Mamó.

"We're the two oldest people on this island," he said. "We were at school together, Mamó and I, though she wasn't called Mamó in those days. When I heard she was near her death, do you know what I felt? That if she were gone, there would be no reason for myself to stay."

"Who would do the weaving?" the doctor asked.

"I'll tell you something, young man," said Manus, and it made me smile to hear him call him by this name when he was surely as old as my own father. "I'll tell you something: there's no one so valuable that they can't be done without. As sure as there's a tail on a cat, there's some young fellow on Inishgillan that knows a bit about the weaving, and he's often thinking to himself that if old Manus Griffin would clear off to heaven, there would be a snug little living waiting here for himself. That's the way of the world, and it's no good trying to go against it."

"There doesn't seem to be a great run on the job of being the doctor."

Manus looked worried.

"I'm not at all pleased with what they did to you," he said. "'Tis a serious thing to keep a man against his will." The doctor brightened up at this, but he sagged again when Manus went on: "But sure, 'tis no good to be fighting fate, and I suppose 'tis your fate to end your days with us. Now I want to tell you that there's always a welcome here for you, and Nora nearly always has the kettle on the boil, and there's nothing I like better than an excuse to give up working for a while. Mamó is the same, she tells me."

"What was her name, before she was called Mamó?"

"Barbara," said Manus. "And she was a beauty. She was like a young half-wild filly, God bless her. We were going to be married, but the little dark man came back from the States with his bag full of money, and her father couldn't resist him. I had only the loom. You'd never starve while you'd have a loom, but you wouldn't grow fat either. I went wandering myself for a year or two after that, and I came back and reared a family of my own. And now myself and Barbara are left, after all, and our two partners are gone to glory."

"Where did you wander?" the doctor asked gently.

"To South America. There was a man from the island going up the Amazon with an expedition. It was all arranged; he had only come home for a small while to say good-bye to his old mother, for fear the cannibals would get him, for they were a wild lot up there in those days. I went along with him."

"Up the Amazon!"

The doctor hitched his chair forward, and in a moment they were so deep in the South American jungle that they hardly heard Nora call them to their tea. It was then that she got out the letter, and the rest of my time was taken up with reading that, and with helping her to guess at whether her son was healthy and rich, and whether he intended to come home soon.

After that evening, the doctor was a different man. His face was no longer twisted into the savage expression which was almost all we had seen on it until now. As Molly had said, one look from him would turn new milk sour. Now he began to look more like an ordinary man, that would stop and chat with you if you met him on the road, maybe, or that would call out a warning to a child that was doing something dangerous. Gradually the men took to dropping in to our house, on their way down to Andy Folan's shop for an evening's talk, and asking the doctor to come along. They asked it as a favour, saying that they would benefit greatly from having a man of knowledge present at their discussions. But lest he might feel that they were including this among his duties as the island's doctor, they always made sure to inquire whether he felt well enough to come. He always said that he did, and we who lived in the same house with him knew that he used to wait eagerly for night to fall, with his chair placed so that he had a clear view from the door of the first men coming down the hill.

At Andy's, he was rather quiet, only giving his view when he was pressed. He would sit in the corner by the counter, with a glass in one hand and his pipe in the other, blinking his eyes as he looked sleepily from one face to another of the men talking. He looked so like a fireside cat that I have never since felt quite at ease with a cat in the room. They have exactly the same air of listening to every word and storing it up for future use. His judgements, when he gave them, were good. It was his word which finally prevented the men from building the pookaun. After he had spoken on it, the subject was never brought up again. What he said was:

"If you build that pookaun, and if it founders in a storm, you'll always have the idea in the back of your minds that the men sailing in her would never have been drowned if you had come by the timber honestly. Now, you don't want to create superstitions that will work against yourselves. You know that there is a good chance that your pookaun will drown. When that happens, you'll have scruples ever afterwards about picking up wrack that floats in from the sea. That wrack is a very useful part of your income. It would be a great deal to pay for one pookaun."

Roddy, beside me, whispered into my ear:

"Isn't that a great mouthful of talk and insults to say he doesn't advise them to build the pookaun?"

"It sounds like good reasoning to me," I said. "That man has a good philosopher's head on him."

And I certainly admired the doctor for that. I had always loved to talk to a man who can take a question to pieces the way you'd card a fleece of wool, or the way you'd sort a catch of fish. I wanted to know how things worked, the engines of a ship, the flashing light on the lighthouse, Manus Griffin's loom. Most of all, as long as I can remember, I had wanted to know how my own body worked, why I could make it do some things and not others, why I felt hungry, or sick, or sore, how many bones I had, and all sorts of other things, that never seemed to trouble other boys at all. Roddy said:

"Isn't it enough for you that it works? You're hungry and you eat, and you're hungry no longer. That should satisfy you. 'Tisn't decent to be wanting to know what goes on in your own stomach. I hope I'll die without ever finding out what goes on in mine."

It was no use talking to him about that sort of thing, and I soon gave it up. But I did not stop thinking of it. The presence of the doctor reminded me every day that there was a great store of knowledge to be had and that I had no possible way of reaching it. I used to watch his head and wish that there was some magic way in which I could see into it and discover what he knew. One evening, he looked up quickly and caught me with my eyes fixed on him.

"What are you thinking of?" he asked abruptly.

"I was thinking of what a fine thing it must be for you to have all that knowledge, and what a hard thing it is for me to be so ignorant."

"You are not ignorant," he said gently, sorry for me, I suppose, because of the bitterness in my voice.

"Oh, I can read and write, and build a currach, and throw a net, make a lobster-pot—that sort of thing. But those are skills your hands could have, even if you hadn't a brain to your name."

"I don't believe it. It takes a clever man to do every one

of those things. And I'm told you were clever at school."

"Who told you?"

"Mamó did. She said you learned to read in half the usual time, and that you could do a sum in your head while the boy beside you would be only thinking of writing it down."

"Mamó thinks well of everyone," I said. "There's no one like her. When we used to vex her at school, talking or jumping around when we were supposed to be quiet, she used to throw a stuffed rabbit at us. She had a great aim too, for a woman. 'Twas a small little toy rabbit, but 'twould sting you if you got it on the ear. And she had a can of sweets in the cupboard, and if you were good, you would always get a sweet. We got one nearly every day, though we were wicked little scalltáns most of the time."

"You would like to learn some of the things that I know?" he asked after a moment's pause.

"I would give my life for it, but sure it's no use talking. You have to go into Galway to learn all those things. Willie O'Connell told me."

"You might learn a bit, if you were to come around with me when I visit the sick people."

"They wouldn't like it, maybe," I said, "a boy coming into their bedroom and they sick."

"I could ask them. If they say no, then you can stay outside. They might get used to you in a while."

They did get used to me. The very next day, when the time came for the doctor to make his round of visits, I was ready to go with him. He put what he thought he would need into his bag and I carried it for him. If it had not been for this, I am sure that many of the patients would have told me that I had no business there and that I should run off and find something useful to do. They have a short enough way with boys on Inishgillan. When they saw me with the bag, naturally they thought that the doctor was either too weak or too much of a gentleman to carry it himself. They made no more objection than if I had been a horse under a cart, overhearing a private conversation.

In this way I came to learn about many of the common diseases that afflict people, and I learned how some of them can be cured and some of them can be made easier to bear even though they can't be cured. As we walked from house to house, the doctor talked to me about all this, and he told me many things about how a healthy body should work, as well. At home, he drew pictures and diagrams for me, and made lists of all the juices that the body manufactures, so that I could hardly swallow my food without seeing in my imagination what was happening to it in my stomach. I got used to that in a while, but we could not talk of such things at meal-times because my mother did not like it. She doubted if God ever meant us to know those things, she said, and it didn't seem right nor proper to be forever discussing them. This was the same idea that Roddy had had, and yet they had been quite anxious to have the doctor, who knew all that was to be known. There's no understanding people that have no curiosity.

More than these things I learned: I stood by the doctor when he operated on Ned Faherty the day he got the sudden pain below at the slip, just when he was setting out for an evening's fishing. Our kitchen table was the operating-table. My poor mother was the nurse. I put Ned to sleep with the little drops out of a bottle of chloroform, that nearly knocked myself out as well. That evening there was a new light in the doctor's eye, and it stayed there long after the excitement had died down. It was easy to see that he was glad to be back to work.

Big John came the next morning and stood in the middle of the kitchen, and made a little speech of thanks for everyone on Inishgillan.

"You owe us nothing," he said, "for we took you against your will. Ned Faherty would be dead this minute but for you, and we want you to know that we are thankful to you from the bottom of our hearts."

From that day onwards, they took him for one of their own, and gave him their trust and confidence in a way that they had never done with a stranger before, in all the history of the island.

Chapter Seven

So it came about that when the time came for sending the spring lambs over to the Grazing Island, the men made no secret of their anxiety when they talked to the doctor. Indeed many of them went out of their way to explain to him exactly how things were, so that he might take part in the conversations that went on endlessly now on this subject. Most of the conferences took place in Andy Folan's shop, and even when the men knew that a conference was planned, still they called for the doctor on their way there, as they did on ordinary evenings. But I noticed that they never asked his advice as to what they should do, and he could not offer it, of course, without being asked.

It was a good year for lambs. Nearly three hundred of them were ready to go, as well as a few stragglers that had been late in arriving in the world.

"'Twould be better to keep them here on short rations than to send them over there to their death," Big John said.

"Their rations would be mighty short," said Simon Conneeley, one of the twins that lived near the slip. "You can see already the way they're nibbling this island clean, and 'tisn't smaller they'll be getting."

"'Tis the mystery I hate," said Sidecar vehemently. "The mystery. That's the queer part of it, that we don't know what's happening to them."

Roddy nudged me so hard with his elbow that I fell off the creepie stool that we were both sitting on. When I did, Roddy's end of the stool went down, and himself with it. We made a great clatter. Everyone turned to look at us. I climbed to my feet, very red in the face, as you may imagine. Roddy was still gathering himself up when I began to speak, for I was anxious not to have it look as if we were jig-acting in the middle of serious business. From the first word, they listened to me.

"We'll stay with the sheep," I said. "Myself and Roddy Hernon. We won't be afraid. Often we planned it between us, that we'd go for the night, and find out what goes on there after darkness falls."

"God save us all," said Sidecar, in the hushed silence. "That would be a brave thing to do."

I felt my spine prickle but I said steadily enough:

"'Tis certain that someone will have to go. If we have plenty of bread and a few candles, and enough turf for the fire—"

"A gallon of milk for the cats, you should have," Sidecar said, "and a bottle of Holy Water."

"We don't believe those old stories," Roddy said boldly.

"You don't? Wasn't my own uncle one of the people that saw those cats, a man that wouldn't tell a lie to save his life!"

"If there is any evil there, it won't touch us," I said quickly, trying to make peace. "We'll bring the Holy Water in any case. Isn't it always in the currachs? If anyone else wants to go instead of us, they're welcome. We're only saying we'll go if no one else wants to go."

There were no volunteers and I could see by the men's faces that there would be none. My father said in a low voice:

"We'll have to ask your mother. Maybe she won't like it."

I had thought of that, indeed, and so had Roddy. But it turned out that we need not have feared that they would prevent us. My mother snorted with contempt when I told her what Sidecar had said.

"A poor little pysawn, that fellow! Afraid of his shadow!" Wouldn't the pooka get him on the road home from Andy's as fast as he would on the Grazing Island? They have no spirit that they wouldn't go out there themselves and keep watch like men, instead of leaving it to two boys."

"Aren't you afraid of the fairies at all?" I asked in wonder, for I had not heard any older person talk like this.

"'Tisn't Christian to be afraid of them," she said. "'Tisn't right nor proper. We all know they're there, but God is above looking down on us, and He won't let them do too much to us. They might make you hurl with them, or dance with them, but who would mind that? 'Tis not much to ask of a person."

Roddy's mother said much the same thing. Roddy told me about it when we met the next morning.

"And she said that if the men would have let her go over in the currach, long ago she would have spent a night on the island herself. But they wouldn't let her go, my father and my uncle. They said it was men's work, but they didn't go themselves either. There was a fierce argument about it last night."

"And does your mother believe that there are fairies there?"

"She does. But she says that a man is always a match for a fairy."

We laughed a lot over that, but soon a date was fixed for the expedition, and then I noticed that as evening came on I always made sure not to walk abroad alone. Sometimes walking with Roddy, I'd hear a rush of little feet behind and turn quickly, but there would be nothing there but the wind blowing the sand along the road. The bleating of a goat after dark sounded like a queer high laugh. In the day-time everything was all right and so long as I was with a crowd of people in a house. But every night I got into a cold sweat as I imagined the moon going down into the sea leaving us alone with the mischievous fairies on the Grazing Island.

The day before we were due to go, my father said:

"Would you like to back out now? There's no one will hold it against you."

He meant it kindly, but I knew in my heart and soul that if we were to back out now, it would never be forgotten for us as long as we would live, nor as long as our grandchildren and great-grandchildren would live either. The men would feel that they had been fooled, even though none of themselves was willing to go.

"We're all ready," I said. "Why would we back out now? 'Twill be a bit of fun."

"God be with the youth of me!" he said in wonder. "I suppose I was like that once myself."

Great preparations had to be made for transporting the sheep to the Grazing Island. As I have said, our currachs are made of canvas stretched tightly over a lath frame and tarred. Sheep have sharp little hooves, and one prod of these would make a hole that would sink the currach while you'd say "cush" to a duck. Long before the expedition used to set out every year, the island women would get out the thick straw mats that they kept for this purpose, and go over them for worn patches and for parts that might have rotted away. Then, on the morning of setting out for the island, these were laid in the currachs, and the sheep, with their feet tied, were loaded on top of them. A calm day was necessary, because the loading had to be done from the slip. It was a delicate enough business, as you may imagine. The water was shallow there, and if the currach overturned, there was always a man standing by to fish out the sheep and lay them up on the slip until the currach was righted again.

Twenty-three currachs went out that day. It was a beautiful, calm morning, with a sea like satin and not a cloud in the sky. The water was so clear that we could look over the side and see the clean rocks with the weed growing on them, away down below us. The sheep cried with fear, as they always did in the currachs, and the miserable sound cut me to the heart so that I almost felt like joining in with them. This, and the heavy, hot smell of their wool, and their meek terrified faces, made me long for the end of that journey, even if it was going to be my last.

I looked across at Roddy's father's boat. There was Roddy sunk in the stern, as I was myself, only occasionally looking over the side to watch a fat rock-fish slip over the floor of the sea. If we could have been together, we might have kept each other's hearts up, but of course, each of us was expected to travel in the family boat, and this was what we did.

The men were very silent too. There was no singing from boat to boat as there usually was when all the boats went out together. Then it was the custom for the men in one boat to sing the first verse of a song, and another to sing the second verse, and so on. That day, Sidecar started up with the "Irish Rover":

> *"In the year of Our Lord, eighteen hundred and six,*
> *We set sail from the fair Cove of Cork—"*

He had got no further than that when Bartley MacDonagh said:

"I'd as soon we had no singing today, Sidecar. I'm not in the humour for it."

"Ho! So when you're not in the humour, there's to be no singing! Maybe the rest of the population feels like a song?"

Any other day, there would have been a shout of support for Sidecar, if it was only to take a rise out of Bartley. Today they just bent to the oars and said not a word. After an uneasy moment, Sidecar got busy with his pipe and pretended to have lost interest.

The boats kept close together, because if anyone was having trouble with his sheep he would need help very quickly. As we passed by the Three Rocks, every man's head was turned to where the *Coriander* had struck, and as we passed Trá Fhada, they all fixed their eyes on the spot where she had gone down. I remembered that I should ask my father to show me the exact spot where she lay. I was probably the only boy on the island who did not know, and all my life it would be a necessary piece of knowledge for me.

Beyond Trá Fhada, there was a smooth rolling swell, not very high, but enough to separate the boats from each other. From my place in the stern of the currach, I was able to see the green curve of the Grazing Island ahead of us, growing greener every moment as we approached it. It was a green unbroken by walls or fences. No one had every troubled to build them, since there was never any reason for separating the animals that grazed there. Otherwise the island was a little like Inishgillan, in that it had a high cliff on the Atlantic side and a sloping, sandy beach on the sheltered side. A small stream ran down through the sand, and a short reef of rocks ran a little way out into the sea. This made a natural slip, because the rocks were worn smooth and flat by the continual beating of the sea.

As our fleet of currachs came close, a few seals, that had been sitting on the end of the reef sunning themselves, plopped off into the water. The tops of their black, shiny heads moved silently along for a while, and disappeared when they dived.

"They're the look-out boys," I heard Sidecar say.

"Quiet," said Big John, with an anxious look at my father in our boat.

He had not heard, however. He was busy watching that his currach should not strike the rocks as she came alongside. In a moment he had leaped ashore and was hauling her in gently by the tow-rope.

Then came the difficult task of lifting out the wretched sheep without allowing them to pierce the currach's sides. A sheep, even a young one, is the most awkward bundle that you ever handled. When we had ours ashore and had untied their feet, we were glad to pull our currach out of the way to make room for the next one, and leave the men in it to deal with their own sheep.

Ours walked stiffly up the rocks until they came to the sand. They crossed that without a moment's hesitation, walking quite fast, as if they had often been here before and knew their way quite well. They reached the green, soft grass above the sand, long, juicy grass that had two months of sweet growth in it, and they started immediately to pull up mouthfuls of it.

"It was high time for them to come, all right," said Roddy at my elbow. "How do you feel?"

"Never better."

This was not true, but I certainly did not feel like telling the truth just then. Roddy's father had got his sheep ashore and was making way for Big John and Sidecar. Roddy nodded towards them and said:

"There's a heap of good advice coming our way, if I'm not mistaken. You'd think Sidecar had spent his whole life holding concourse with the fairies."

"Maybe he did."

"Maybe, indeed, but I'm thinking what he really wants is to know if we are really afraid and covering it up very well."

Sure enough, in a few moments Sidecar was beside us, peering from one of us to the other anxiously and saying:

"Will ye be all right now? Are ye sure ye're not afraid now?"

"We won't be a bit afraid, so long as you stay with us yourself, Sidecar," said Roddy solemnly.

Sidecar looked quickly around to see if anyone had overheard this. When he saw that they had not, he leaned in closer and said:

"I can't stay, agrá. I'd like to, indeed, but the old woman at home do be nervous. She can't sleep a wink if I'm not there beside her. God help us. I didn't tell her I might be out the night, and if she got the message she'd never believe it. She'd swear 'twas drowned I was and that they were afraid to tell her."

It was one of Sidecar's peculiarities that he imagined that his wife could not live without him. This was handy enough, since she had the same notion about him. We used to laugh at them then, but I have often thought since that they were really devoted to each other, and this was their way of apologising or explaining it to the rest of the islanders.

Roddy said now:

"Don't worry your head, Sidecar. We'll be fine. There's nothing to be afraid of."

Sidecar lowered his voice still further.

"There's something to be afraid of, all right, though it may not be fairies. Don't forget, those sheep are disappearing. If the fairies don't take them, where do they go?"

He moved away from us and we had no more talk with him, but he had put a nasty idea at work in our heads. We had been so busy scoffing at the notion of fairies that we had given very little thought to what else we might meet. Rather desolately we watched while the currachs were put to sea again. My father and Roddy's were the last to go. My father said:

"Keep your eyes and your ears open. As long as there's two of you, 'tis all right. They won't harm you. We'd get the Guards out from Galway only that they'd poke into everything while they'd be at it. There's no sense in drawing those fellows on us. Some of them come from the Midlands, where there isn't a boat nor a sea for forty or fifty miles. What do they know about people like us?"

"Ay, 'tis best to be our own guards," said Roddy's father. "You'll have a blessing for it."

Just before pushing off, Big John told Sidecar to hold

on to the rocks for a moment. He stepped ashore and came over to say to us:

"Make sure to see their faces. That's the most important thing. And keep out of sight. We'll be here for you at noon tomorrow."

In complete silence we watched them row away. The sea had risen a little and it seemed to us that the following wind took them away from the island a lot faster than we had approached it.

When they had become so small that we could no longer tell one man from another, somehow we did not want to look at them any more. We turned away and followed the track of the sheep, walking through the soft grass, carrying our bag of turf, and an old blanket and our provisions.

Once we were on the grass, our bare feet moved without a sound. Then the sounds of the island suddenly seemed to fill the air like thunder, though each one was small in itself. From the sea came the wash of the waves. Above our heads, the larks sang, a sound too sweet for this world. Down by the shore the seagulls quarrelled. The wind raced up over the island with a roar and a whistle. All around us the little teeth of the sheep nibbled and nibbled. Among all those sounds, it seemed to us suddenly the loneliest place in the whole world.

Without a word to each other, we made for the bothán that was to house us for the night. It was not a real house, for no one had ever lived the year round on this island. It was built of sods cut from the surrounding grassy ground by some Inishgillan man, long dead. The sods had grown together with the years and had become indistinguishable from each other, so that but for the thatched roof the bothán might have been a little hollow green hill. The straw of the thatch was dark brown with age except where the grass had begun to grow over it. Inside, it was as dark as a cave. The only light came through the open doorway. There was no chimney. Anyone wanting a fire was expected to light it outside, and several big flat stones had been laid before the doorway for this purpose.

The house looked very snug to us. We laid the old blanket out on the earth floor. Then we set about making a fire. As soon as the smoke began to flow up from it, instantly we felt more easy. I have noticed that it always happens like this, that when you have a fire, you have home.

We had bread and bacon with us, which we ate then, in the middle of the day. We had water from the stream to wash it down with. By the time we had got as far as that, the fire had made plenty of hot brown ash, and we buried some potatoes in that. There they would cook very slowly, and be ready for our supper in a few hours' time. We covered as much of the fire as we could with ashes, and hoped that a strong wind would not blow up and sweep them all away. The hearth was sheltered by the little house, as well as by a big rock at one side of it, so it would be bad luck if this were to happen.

Leaving the remainder of our property in the house, we set out to walk the island. Already the sheep were dotted all over it. They were so happy to be filling their stomachs that they had forgotten the fears and pains of the journey over. They hardly turned their silly heads as we passed by, and it occurred to me that they must be the easiest of animals to steal. They seem to have no natural Christian feelings at all, the way a horse does, or a dog, or even a goat. That afternoon it was clear that they were not interested in us. They just nibbled and gobbled as if they never hoped to get a decent bit again, taking a few steps and then a few more steps, never lifting their eyes to look around them.

"'Tis grand to be here alone," Roddy said suddenly. "No one to give us orders, no one to tell us when to go to bed, when to get up—"

"No one to cook our supper."

"We can do that ourselves. No plates to wash up, for we'll eat out of the skins. 'Tis a great life."

We raced each other to the high cliff and stood there in the wind looking north, south, east and west. There was Inishgillan with smoke coming up from the houses, blowing away off to the north. There was Inishthorav, with smoke blowing towards us. It was a lower island than ours, without any cliffs and with no cells of saints either. Saints did live there once, but the name Inishthorav means the "Bull's Island", and our men used to laugh at theirs for having no saint but a bull only. That kind of thing makes bad neighbours, as I found out afterwards.

Farther off than Inishthorav we could see Inishbofin, which means the "island of the fair cow." That is surely as poor a name as Inishthorav, but since the people there were farther away, we did not trouble much with teasing them. Besides, Bofin is a big island, almost like the biggest Aran island, which made it rather independent of what we might think of it. And of course it has the cells of many saints to boast of.

We walked downhill again, past the rocky gully which led with a sudden drop to the stones at the foot of the cliff. There was room for a sheep to get through there, and fall to her death on the beach, but as Roddy pointed out, she would have to climb over a rock as big as herself to get to the dangerous place.

"Sheep are fools," he said, "but they're not so foolish as to do that. If you watch them, you'll see that they walk around an obstacle rather than climb over it. And there's nothing for them down there, to tempt them into the gully. And their bodies were never found there."

We made the whole round of the island, with some idea, I suppose, of making sure that we were alone on it with the sheep. There was no doubt of that, but still as evening came on we began to be very uneasy.

"I wish the sunset would hold off another while," Roddy said as we watched it, a beautiful panorama of gold and orange and indigo.

"They should never talk of fairies, the old ones," I said. "If we had never heard of them, we wouldn't be afraid of them."

When darkness fell, we sat just inside the bothán one at either side of the doorway. It would have been a comfort to have made the fire blaze up, but we could not afford to waste our turf. If we did, we'd have had none for the next morning, when we would surely be glad of it after our night's vigil. Also, the things that Big John had said before he went away had given us the idea that the men were thinking of something quite different from fairies. What is the use of keeping out of sight when the fairies are around? Don't they know exactly where to poke you out? And what is the use of seeing a fairy's face? There's some that say they have seen them and that they look sad and sometimes very old, or they'll tell you that fairies have green eyes and pale, pale cheeks. But it was not for that kind of information we had come to the Grazing Island.

When the moon rose, the grass looked black as soot.

Out there we could hear the sheep's teeth still nibbling. Higher and higher the moon went, with a shimmering path going straight from it across the sea and right to where we sat. Along that path I could well believe that a host of fairies would come twirling and dancing, gabbling amongst themselves as they are said to do, and planning mischief and villainy on the poor people of this world. But though we stared a long time, not a move did we see, not a cat, not a seal, not any sign of that eerie life that is the whole substance of the old people's stories.

We talked a little between ourselves, but there was not much that we wanted to say, nothing that could not wait until the morning. Still it was necessary for us to talk, for as time went on, we were inclined to doze off in spite of ourselves. Presently I know that I slept, for I awoke to find the moon utterly gone and Roddy clutching my shoulder. His mouth was close to my ear, and I could feel his breath tickle me.

"Don't make a sound. There's someone out there."

I put my mouth to his ear to ask:

"Who?"

"I don't know. I heard a man laugh softly."

My skin prickled. Why should a man laugh on an empty island, unless he was some strange being?

"I'll tell you the class of a fairy he is," Roddy's voice said again close into my ear, as if he had guessed my thought. "He came in a currach. I think there's two of them there."

I felt so relieved that I would have gone out and fought them single-handed. Roddy warned me again:

"Be quiet. He has gone along the island a piece. The other one stayed with the currach. We could maybe watch them a bit, without being seen."

"'Tis too dark."

"There's a sky of moon," he said, which is our way of describing the light that remains when the moon is gone. "It looks dark in here, with the rock and the house cutting out the light. Out there it's brighter."

"Who are they?"

"That's what I want to know."

"They may see us."

"They may, indeed, but we can go to a lot of trouble to prevent it."

This was what we did, sliding along almost on our stomachs over the wet, dewy grass, slipping behind the few grass-grown rocks that made patches of shadow here and there. In one of these I said:

"I wonder what time would it be?"

"About midnight. The moon is not long gone."

"Did you sleep?"

"No. I was wishing we had a knife or a harpoon, same, to protect ourselves with. I asked my father to leave us the like, but he wouldn't."

"My father wouldn't either," I said. "He told me that if you strike once, your enemy will strike twice. 'Tis sense, I suppose, but somehow you feel stronger when you have a knife in your hand."

"I'm thinking they didn't want us to feel strong. A strong man goes looking for fight. We're only here to see what's to be seen."

Neither of us wanted to say that if we were discovered and if the night-walkers on the island were desperate enough, we might never be seen again. Roddy felt for my hand and gripped it for a moment. Then he said into my ear:

"The man that laughed went up over the shoulder of

the island. He has no idea there's anyone here but the two of themselves. If he had, he would have been quieter. I'm sure of that."

"He wasn't afraid of the fairies," I said sourly, remembering my terror of a few hours ago.

We peered around the rocks, hoping to catch a sight of him. The place where we lay hidden was rather high on the hill, so that we could look away down from it to the sea. Then as we watched, fifty yards lower down the hill we heard a high, thin whistle. The man's head appeared above the line of the hill, and he grew taller and taller as he came over the curve of it. He whistled again. We heard the light drumming of hooves and a short, happy bark. Then along came a little huddled flock of six sheep. A dog circled them around and around keeping them together as closely as if they were in a pen at Galway Fair. The man walked ahead, quite unconcerned, obviously trusting his good dog to do the work for him. It seemed to me a terrible thing that such a good dog as this should be made a party to thieving and meanness.

"That's a great dog," Roddy said into my ear.

Though he was so far away, the dog stopped and lifted his head, half-turning in our direction. Then he came galloping up the hill to sniff at us, with tiny whinnies and barks, so soft that they were more like grunts. The man had walked on several paces before he noticed that the sheep were no longer running behind him. He stopped and looked all around him, and we could imagine him peering blindly into the gloom.

Roddy said to the dog, in a whisper:

"Get off! Get off home! Go on with you!"

Still the dog snuffled around us. The man lifted his chin and let out a clear, high whistle. Then he called:

"Here, Shep! Shep!"

And he whistled again. This time the dog could not resist him, he had been so well trained. With his tail and his muzzle down, he ran flatly down the hill, with all the airy spring gone out of him, as if to show how much he hated being called back to work.

With a few more whistles, the man had him rounding up the sheep again. When the dog had collected them, this time the man walked behind the little group as they went down towards the sea.

I felt myself cold all over and shaking with fright. My breath came in uneven gasps to my lungs, so that my chest was sore. For a few minutes neither of us could speak. Then Roddy said:

"'Twas only an old dog."

"I thought 'twas a tiger," I said. "We're a nice pair, and no mistake. We got out of that well."

"We're not out of it yet," Roddy said. "Did you recognise his voice?"

Again I heard in my imagination the voice of the man calling the dog.

"'Twas no one from our island," I said, "but 'twas like an island man for all that. Did you recognise him?"

"Not for certain sure, and that's what we'll have to do. We'll have to see his face."

"How can we do that? He's gone away down to the sea."

"It will take him time to load the sheep into the currach. One at a time they'll have to go, and the matting will have to be secure. They won't take any chances. We'll be around by the currach before they are ready to go to sea."

We slipped out of the shadow of the rock and began

to crawl back by the way that we had come. There was need to hurry, as we knew, because the moonlight would not last for ever. Without it we would see nothing, of course, for even if we had a light, we would not have dared to flash it on the thieves' faces.

We passed by the bothán and went down to the sea, and came out onto the shore a good thirty yards west of the reef which served as a slip, from which we had landed earlier. From that distance, we could hear how the feet of the sheep rolled the stones nervously about. The dog was very excited, jumping around them on his hind legs. Now we saw the second man in silhouette, bent double on the reef, holding his currach in close. The men hardly spoke to each other at all, and they had an air of having worked together often, they needed so little to give each other directions. One by one, the man on the beach spancelled the sheeps' legs together and lifted them into the currach. We risked a great deal in moving gradually closer and closer, but we were determined that we would not let them leave the island unidentified.

Then, suddenly Roddy lay flat on the grass, as flat as a worm, or an old sack. I did the same. Now we wished heartily that we were not so close to the reef, but it was too late to wish for anything but that some miracle would save us. In the short time since we had seen the first man, we had concluded that he was an innocent. He never looked behind him, nor made any attempt to scour the ground around him, so sure he was that he was alone but for his friend and the dog and the sheep. What we had seen was that two more currachs were approaching the reef. It would be a miracle indeed if six men and three dogs were all so unsuspicious.

We were near enough to hear them talk to each other,

quite without fear. As they came close in, the man in the first currach called out:

"Hóra, Mike Rua!"

"Hóigh, Patcheen Bill!" the man on the shore answered.

"You're ready to go?" the first man said.

"I am, faith, and a fine present with me from the men of Inishgillan."

"They're always decent with the sheep," said the first man, and he laughed heartily.

"No so much noise," said the man who had loaded his sheep. "'Tis true there isn't a soul here but ourselves, and still I'm uneasy tonight, for some reason. And Shep is uneasy. I can feel him shivering, what he never does."

"Give him a fine glass of whiskey when you get him home," said the first man, who had his currach alongside by now. "In no time at all, he'll be talking about his mother's people."

The third currach was close enough for the men in her to have heard this. There was a general laugh from all the men. The man who had reached the island first said:

"Well, we're ready to go, and glad I am to be off. I'd be glad to be safe in Inishthorav this minute and that's no lie."

The others jeered a bit at him and he and his friend cast off and began to row carefully with their awkward cargo, out into the darkness of the sea. But when they were left alone, the four remaining men were quieter. They wasted no time, but set off with their dogs to round up some sheep.

Still we lay there, chilled and terrified, until presently the moonlight left the sky and a heavy darkness fell like a curtain over the island. We dared not move or speak, lest one of the dogs might draw attention to us, but it was good to know that we couldn't be seen. After more than an hour, the two currachs had cast off, and the sound of their dipping oars had almost died away in the still air.

Roddy rolled over cautiously and said:

"There may be more of them coming. How do we know? They could be coming all night."

"'Tis too dark now," I said. "They won't come back until tomorrow night. Eighteen sheep! 'Tis like murder! And to have to stand by and let them go!"

"We didn't stand, that's one sure thing," said Roddy.

He got up and began to jump around to get warm.

"You sound mighty cheerful," I said. "I could do murder tonight myself. The scoundrels! Our own neighbours!"

"Well, now we know where the sheep are gone, and we know the names of the men that took them. We did what we came to do, and we have news. Oh! We have news for the men in the morning!"

Though we were sure that no more of the Inishthorav men would come for sheep, still we did not dare to make the fire blaze in the darkness. On their way home, we thought, they might glance back and see it. A fire can be seen across the sea for a long distance. We went back to the bothán and wrapped ourselves in the rug, and there we sat close together, half dozing, and waiting for the dawn.

Chapter Eight

As soon as it was daylight, we raked out our fire from the ashes and put fresh sods on it. When these had caught fire, we piled on more and more recklessly, until we had a great round blazing fire shaped like a volcano. There was a bitter nip in the early morning air. We moved in as close to the fire as we dared, and warmed ourselves while we heated water for tea. It was my mother who had insisted that we bring tea with us, and we drank it gladly, hot and strong. Fortunately for us, some ewes had been brought with the lambs, so we were able to have sheep's milk in it.

The sheep seemed contented this morning. They had stopped eating, for a wonder, and were sitting about on the dewy grass looking thoughtful. Many a time I have wished I knew what sheep were thinking of, but never so much as that morning. Did they miss their eighteen companions? Were they worrying lest they too might go the same road? Did they have anything at all in their heads, beyond a few wisps of grass that they had forgotten to swallow? It was exasperating to watch them, and I turned impatiently away.

In the white dawn, the sea was smooth and calm. The

swell seemed to have gone down. A little mist hung over the grass here and there. We were very quiet, for our heads were heavy from lack of sleep and it seemed too much work even to speak. We sat one at either side of the fire, savouring the heat of it, and I believe that if Manannán Mac Lir himself had walked up out of the sea to us, we would only have lifted an eyebrow at him.

Noon seemed an age away, when the men would come to take us off the island. After a while, I persuaded Roddy to go into the bothán to sleep. He kept on saying that he would not, until at last I spread the blanket for him and led him by the arm in there, to lie on it. I think the very sight of it made him fall asleep before he had even lain down. I stood there watching him stretched out and I grudged him his comfort sorely. Still I knew that we could not both sleep, and that he had been awake the whole night through, while I had slept in the early part of it.

I walked by myself all over the island, to keep awake, and went down at last to the slip. I walked into the shallow edge of the sea, which was cold enough to sting my toes. All around me there were footmarks, but these could have been made by our own men yesterday. The Inishthorav men wear rawhide shoes, as we do, so there was no way of telling them apart. After a while, however, I saw the tracks of dogs' paws on a patch of mud at the mouth of the stream. I could tell them by their shape as well as by the fact that they were always a little away from the other tracks. This was because of the way in which the dogs had circled around the little flock of sheep. It was only then that I found the tracks of smaller bare feet. This could only mean that there had been a boy in last night's party, though we had been lying too low to see him. A fine thing, I thought, to be such an accomplished thief at so young an age.

The men arrived punctually at noon. Long before that I had awakened Roddy, for I was unable any longer to tolerate the loneliness of the island. As soon as we saw the Inishgillan currach coming, we rolled up our blanket and scattered our fire, and ate the remainder of our food. Then we went down to the slip to wait for the currach to touch land.

My father and Roddy's father had a pair of oars each. While they were still far out at sea, we shouted and waved to them, to show that we were alive and well. They hopped ashore like boys, they were in such a hurry to hear our story.

"Well, what did ye see?"

"Not cats, not fairies, but men and dogs. The men of Inishthorav came last night and stole eighteen sheep. They took them away in their currachs."

"How many currachs?"

"Three, six sheep to a currach."

"Did they see you? Did you try to stop them?"

"No, no. We stayed quiet, hiding in the shadows. A dog sniffed at us but he didn't tell on us."

"God look down on us all! The men of Inishthorav! Our own neighbours!"

"We always knew they don't love us," I said, "and we don't give them much cause to."

"What cause? Do we steal their sheep?"

"No, but I've heard tell of fights in Galway at the fairs, and bargains over cattle that were broken— things of that kind."

"You've heard too much," said Roddy's father. "Boys have no business to be listening to that class of talk."

"But they're all right for watching all night on islands where there might be pookas and fairies of all descriptions—"

"Now, now," said my father soothingly. "We musn't fall out between ourselves. 'Tis true what the boy said, that we didn't give the Inishthorav people cause to love us. But we never did them the kind of injury that they have just done to us. Show us where they landed."

We showed them the tracks of the dogs, and told them how we had lain on the ground when the two new currachs had arrived, and how we had heard the names of Mike Rua and Patcheen Bill called out.

"And if they deny that they were here, we can't prove it any better than that," I said, "for we never saw their faces at all. We were afraid to go too close."

"'Tis proof enough, and a great night's work," said Roddy's father, anxious to make amends for what he had said in anger a few minutes before.

Without knowing why I did it, I steered them away from the footprints left by the boy. There was no more to be done on the island. We loaded our things into the currach and got aboard her, and pushed off. We watched the island fade from green to grey as we moved further and further away from it. I was never so glad to see the last of any place as I was of that island.

As we approached our own slip, we saw that a little crowd was gathered there. Someone had seen us coming and had sent the word around that the news was on the way. They were rather silent, and we noticed that they looked us over as we stepped ashore, to see, I suppose, if the fairies had afflicted us in any way. I was almost sorry that we had not arranged to tell them a good yarn, to give them value, but it was too late when I thought of it, and in any case the men would never have agreed to it. We could have made up a story of sheep dancing in the moonlight to strange fairy music, or seals coming ashore and turning into men.

While I was thinking of this, Big John said with a grin, looking down into the currach:

"If you tell us you saw the fairies, we won't believe a word of it, so you can save your breath."

He held the gunwale while we stepped ashore. We walked up onto the strand, and there in the middle of a silent ring of men, we told our story for the second time. Big John Moran was the first to speak.

"'Tis what we suspected. How sure they are that we won't bring out the Guards from Galway."

"They know well that we don't like the Guards. They don't like them either. 'Twould nearly be worth it."

But a growl went around which denied this.

Sidecar said, stuttering in his eagerness:

"In the old times 'twould never have been tolerated. That's for sure and certain. In the old times, the men of this island would have gone over there, armed to the teeth with guns and knives and pikes, and they would have sacked Inishthorav! That's what they'd have done."

He looked around sharply from face to face, to see if he had aroused their anger. Big John said:

"Times are different now. There's only three guns on this island, that I know of. You can't arm us all to the teeth with three guns. And anyway, those guns are for shooting seals, and rabbits. 'Tis unchristian to talk of turning them against our neighbours."

"Faith, 'tis mighty unchristian to steal your neighbour's sheep. That's in the penny Catechism."

This time Sidecar got a growl of agreement, which encouraged him to add:

"And there's Christian things we could do, turning the other cheek as they say, like sending them over a batch of sheep every few weeks until ours would be all gone and the Inishthorav men would be so fat that the taxing-master would be after them to know did they find a crock of gold or what. It seems to me that Christians weren't meant to keep on turning the other cheek until the head is knocked off them."

"I never said they should," said Big John. "We'll have to teach some Christian manners to the Inishthorav men. We know that. What we don't know is the best way to do it. Old or young, we're not short of courage. When we couldn't go spying on the Grazing Island, for fear of being recognised, we had no bother in finding two powerful boys, with the courage of lions, to do it for us."

Suddenly everyone was cheering us. We stood there, blushing and looking at our toes, and feeling very modest. Big John said to us kindly:

"Off home with ye now, and tell your mothers that you're safe and sound." He turned his shoulder to us and said to the men: "We'd best go up to Andy's place where we can do our planning in comfort. This is going to take time."

And in that moment it seemed that we were forgotten. Not a man glanced back to see if we were going home, as Big John advised us. Not a man asked had we a thirst for lemonade on us. That is the way always in the islands. They believe that if boys are not well kept down, they soon become maneens, which is their word for a boy that is full of his own importance.

Standing there on the slip when they had gone, Roddy laughed shortly and said:

"There's no fear we'll get a swelled head, anyway. I'm

thinking that if we came back with a couple of tails on us, a present from the fairies, they'd have said we were only looking for notice."

"I'm glad nothing of the kind happened," I said.

We were reluctant to straggle after the men, for this would have made us feel even smaller than we did. We walked along the shore and climbed the hill that looked down on the Black Rocks, where the *Coriander* had struck. The rocks had patches of bright orange lichen, which shone like little lamps. The tide was out and we could see the soft yellow sand that was always there. This sand was made of broken shells washed in and smashed up by violent seas. Sometimes a few shells escaped. There was a special kind that I wanted to get for my mother, to decorate the dresser. It was huge and pink, and shaped rather like a periwinkle. They were very rare, but I never passed by the Black Rocks without hoping to see one. It was several years later that I did find one, half-buried in the sand, but on that day that we came back from the Grazing Island I went down as usual to have a search. Roddy followed more slowly. We were both half-asleep, I think, but we were reluctant to go home and be bundled into bed by our mothers, as we knew would be certain to happen.

We were leaning against the landward side of the innermost rock, looking vaguely about the sand for my shell, when at the same moment we both saw a currach approaching from the north-east. A small, slight figure was using the oars with difficulty and slowly, as if he were tired. Then, while we watched, suddenly he turned the nose of the currach in towards the beach where we were.

Flattened against the rock, we saw him land and pull

the currach above the water-line. Then he stood beside it for a full minute, perfectly still, as if he were waiting for something to happen. We could see his face now, and it was strange to us, though he wore an island jersey.

Suddenly I guessed who he was. I leaped out of hiding, calling to Roddy to help me, and threw myself on the strange boy. A second later, Roddy came pounding after me. Together we overpowered him easily and rolled him over on the soft sand. We held him there so that he could not move. He had made no sound. Now he gazed up at us, his eyes sparkling with rage and his mouth twisted downwards.

"Spying!" I said. "Ha! We know the likes of you, coming around quietly where you thought no one would catch you. A decent man would go in to the slip, but a thief would land on the strand."

"Ye have a name for hospitality on Inishgillan, sure enough," said the strange boy through his teeth. "'Tis said of ye rightly that if any stranger has the misfortune to land here, that he might as well say good-bye to the world, for the Inishgillan men will take the clothes off his back and the holy medal from around his neck—"

"'Tis a lie," said Roddy fiercely.

We released our hold of him a little, feeling rather ashamed of the reception we had given him. He lay there without attempting to get up, fearing, I suppose, that we would leap on him again at his first move. After a moment I asked more civilly:

"What brings you here? Where do you come from?"

"I come from Inishthorav," he said, and he went on hurriedly when he saw our faces blacken: "I came to do ye a good turn, but I'm thinking now that I made a mistake and I'd best be going home if ye'll take your hands off me."

Abruptly I asked:

"Were you on the Grazing Island last night?"

He gaped at me.

"How do you know that?"

"We were there ourselves. We saw you!"

"You did not!" he said quickly, picking up Roddy's start of surprise on its way to me.

"We saw your footprints," I said impatiently. "It's the same thing."

"I was there," he said slowly. "When I went for the first time last year I didn't know what was going to be done there. Then I thought they would only take the sheep one summer, but this year when they started going back, they were talking of next year's loot and the year after's. I said no word to anyone but came over here in the currach to see would I meet someone that I would tell about it."

"You were going to tell about your own people?"

We were shocked at this. Though we believed by now that all Inishthorav people were steeped in wickedness, still it seemed like common sense for them to stick together.

"They're mad," he said in a low voice. "They don't know what they're doing. They don't call it stealing at all, for they have it fixed in their heads that anything they do against the Inishgillan men is a good thing. And if we don't put a stop to it, your grandsons and mine will be fighting in the self-same way, in fifty years from now."

"What is your name?" I asked after a pause.

"Colman Cooney. They call me Colm."

He sat up and we had our first real look at him. He was thin and his hair grew in thick black curls all over his head. He was a year or two younger than we were, about fourteen years old, but his chin stuck out like a grown man's and his blue eyes were hard.

"For more than a year I've been watching them. My own uncle is one of them. If my father were alive, they wouldn't do these things."

"Was your father King Cooney?"

"Yes, and since he died last year, there's no law nor order on Inishthorav. Fights there were in his time between your people and mine, and no love lost, but they never were the way they are now. When they come back with the lambs from the Grazing Island, they hold a big feast, like a lot of pirates. They'll come to no good if this doesn't stop. The Inishgillan men won't have patience for ever. Any day now, they'll be coming over to murder us all, and small blame to them."

At that moment it occurred to me to wonder if Colm had been sent over by the Inishthorav men to find out how much we knew and whether we were planning revenge. Almost at once, however, I decided that this could not be. He looked too honest. Besides, he had sounded angry, and it seemed to me that it would be almost impossible to pretend to be as angry as that.

"'Tis true that the people are getting cross," I said, "but what they're planning I don't know, nor how we can put a stop to them." I looked over Colm's head at Roddy. "We'd best go up and have a word with Mamó. She'll maybe know what can be done."

"If she doesn't, no one will."

We carried the currach above the high-water mark and turned it upside down, to look as if it had a right to be there. Then we went around by the shore path and climbed the hill to Mamó's house, following exactly the way that we had taken with the doctor, on the evening of the wreck. There was no need to tell Colm to keep out of sight, for he seemed quite frightened at finding himself on Inishgillan. He kept his head well down and he ran across open spaces, bent double. Indeed, if anyone had seen him, they would have been mighty suspicious, for he was so obviously keeping under cover.

Coming near to Mamó's house, the smell of her dinner came down the road to meet us. We stopped and looked at each other.

"Dinner-time, of course," I said. "We'll have to go home."

"Ten minutes will do us here," Roddy said. "Once we go in home, the Lord only knows when we'll get out again. I'd swear my mother has a pig's ear for me. She was promising a great treat for dinner today, when I was going off to the island yesterday. She knows I do love a pig's ear."

"They'll be expecting us, for sure."

All at once I had noticed how Colm's face had filled with longing at the mention of the pig's ear. I seized him by the arm and said:

"Five miles over the sea, all alone in the currach! You must have a mighty hunger on you. Come in with you now, and Mamó will give you a piece of her dinner, and you can tell her your story. We'll go home, and we'll come out again after dinner by hook or by crook."

Mention of dinner had pleased him, as I could see, but still he did not make straight for Mamó's house.

"It's all right," I said. "You'll be safe with her. She's well used to keeping secrets. We can ask her to hide you in the room, if anyone comes in."

By this time she was watching us over the half-door. I went across to her and asked:

"Have you enough dinner for two?"

"I have, faith. Who is he?"

"Colm Cooney from Inishthorav. You heard what happened last night?"

"I did. I ran down to Andy Folan's place while the spuds were boiling and I heard it all. What's that boy doing here?"

"He came to help us," I said. "He'll tell you all about it."

"I never liked an Inishthorav man," she said.

"He's not a man, he's a boy."

"'Tis true for you, of course. And to be sure, he looks hungry. Let ye come back quickly."

We watched them both go into the house, with great doubts as to how she would treat him. Then Roddy said:

"It will be all right. Anyone that eats her dinner, she has to love them ever after. We'd better hurry back, though. Pick up all the news you can while you're at home. I'll do the same."

"And keep out of bed!"

That was my last advice to him as I left him at my own door.

I got a great welcome from my mother, and a great dinner too. She sat with me while I ate, and questioned me closely about what had happened on the Grazing Island. She seemed very disappointed that I had seen no enchanted cats, nor goats, nor fairies of any description.

"Didn't you have any company at all at the fire?" she asked.

"Only the two of ourselves. We didn't have a big fire, because we were afraid it would be seen."

"That's why they didn't come, then," she said. "They say that they always like a good fire. That's what draws them, a good fire and a pot boiling on it."

"Where is everyone?" I asked when I could eat no more. I knew well where they were, but I was working around slowly to joining them.

"Below in Andy's shop," my mother said. "There's going to be trouble. They're saying they won't let the Inishthorav men get away with robbery so easy."

"Where is the doctor?"

"He went with them."

"They didn't tell him to keep away?"

She looked quite shocked.

"Oh, no! That would be very bad manners. Isn't he one of our own now? He can give good advice too, being a travelled man."

"Did they come for him?"

"Of course."

"Is he well?"

Since I spent so much time with the doctor, I felt responsible for him and especially for his health.

"Never better," my mother said. "He takes a great interest in all the business of Inishgillan. Very soon he'll be like an island man born and bred. And it takes him out of himself. He's eating better in the last few days, and sleeping better too, I'm thinking. At least, he doesn't look as tired in the mornings as he used to do."

Mention of being tired made her think of my lost night's sleep, and she started in on trying to persuade me to go to bed for the rest of the day. At first I said I had slept enough, but she answered that I had black circles around my eyes. Then I said that I did not feel tired, but she said she knew by the look of me that I did, and that a sleep of a few hours was just what I needed. When I saw that nothing else would serve me, I stood up and said:

"Tell me honestly, Mother: would you like to have a son that would climb into bed for a fine, comfortable sleep, while below in Andy Folan's shop they're talking and discoursing about ways and means for stopping the Inishthorav men?"

"'Tis true, agrá, I wouldn't like it a bit. You'd be a softie, and you'd be drowned for certain sure before you'd be twenty, God save the mark!"

"Amen," said I, making for the door.

"Be sure and remember every word you hear, and come back and tell me," she called after me as I ran down the road.

At first I had intended to circle around behind the houses and go back up to Mamó's at once. But then I thought I might as well drop in to Andy's and find out what was happening there, especially as I might be questioned about it at home later on.

It was well on in the afternoon by now. Outside Andy's door, a pile of shovels and forks laid against the wall showed that the men had all come in from the fields for the meeting. Looking down towards the sea, I could guess that we were in for a spell of fine, windless weather. The sky had only a few clouds, and they were long and thin, rather fish-shaped, which was a sure sign of a calm. This would mean that a raid on Inishthorav would be possible, though indeed it crossed my mind that the men might attempt it in any weather, they were so angry. Peering into the shop over their shoulders, I could see how their eyes flashed and glared, and they muttered angrily to each other without ceasing.

My father, Bartley MacDonagh and Big John Moran were consulting together by the fire. Even without knowing what they were saying, I could tell that they were the real planners, and that the rest of the men would do as they said. We have never had a king on Inishgillan, as they had on many of the islands around. But as far back as anyone could remember, there had always been one or two men who by their natural powers of intelligence and personality had come to be regarded as our leaders in any crisis that affected us all. When this happened, their decisions were usually followed as closely as if they had been real kings.

I looked out for the doctor, and saw him sitting at the very end of the counter, talking to Luke Hernon. They seemed to be not quite part of the counsel by the fire, and yet from time to time Bartley or my father would lean across and say a word to them. I edged in, pushing past the packed backs of the men, making my way gradually around by the wall, until I came to the fireplace. The air was thick with smoke, because all of the men had their pipes going and in times of excitement they always pulled on them and blew out the smoke twice as fast as usual.

I stayed in the recess of the bedroom door, by the fireplace, and hoped that I would not be sent home. All of the looks turned on me were friendly, and rather admiring, indeed, for though they would have been fierce enough in times a real battle, few of these men would have spent a night on an island with a reputation like that of the Grazing Island. I enjoyed those looks. It is pleasant enough to be a hero when one is at a safe distance from the event.

Bartley called out suddenly:

"Now, men! Quiet and hear what Big John has to say."

Silence fell like a curtain, and it was so still that I could hear the pipes bubble as the men drew on them quickly. Big John's voice was not loud.

"We're driven too far. We're peaceful, quiet, God-fearing people on Inishgillan, and have always been. We never injure a neighbour and we never go looking for fight, but by the Holy Wood, we're driven too far this time!"

The men growled angrily but they said nothing.

"You know we can't let our sheep go without a blow struck to save them," Big John went on. "You know there's hardly a man here present that hasn't had at least one sheep stolen by the men of Inishthorav. Are we going to stand for that?"

"No! No, by my hand! No!"

This time the voices were louder. Big John said:

"There's some were suggesting that we should arm ourselves with guns and pikes, and sack Inishthorav. What would that mean? That we'd burn their houses, maybe, or did he mean us to kill the Inishthorav men? We couldn't do that, for it wouldn't be Christian. Wait!" The growling that had started died down again. "What we can do is this: we can get into our currachs tonight. 'Twill be a night of calm, and you can trust me to know that. We can row over to Inishthorav and land there, and take our sheep home with us again. 'Tis a simple idea, you might think, and maybe you might think it's too simple. But we don't. I can tell you why. We have more currachs and more men than they have on Inishthorav. The difference is not much, but it is enough. The second thing is that we'll surprise them, and that will be our biggest advantage. Everyone knows that surprise is half the battle. We're hoping that this won't come to a battle, but if it does, let no man do more injury than he must. Remember always that these are our neighbours, and as we have learned in our catechism at school, our neighbour is all mankind, even those that injure us."

Big John paused and looked around slowly at the men. This time there was no growl. Their faces were all serious and solemn while they contemplated Big John's words. I saw the doctor looking around too, and while I watched him, a little smile moved on his face for a moment and was gone again. I remember thinking:

"It may seem a small thing to you to lose your sheep, Doctor, but if you lived as near to the bone as we do, a sheep would look very important indeed, and maybe even worth killing for."

Then I blamed myself for having read his smile as being superior or contemptuous. It could just as easily have been sympathetic. Big John said:

"Well, what do you say?"

"We'll go and get them back."

"We'll just give them a taste of their own medicine."

"'Tis the easy way, and the right way, just to take them back."

"And you won't strike a blow at any of the Inishthorav men?" Big John said.

"No, not a blow," said all the men with resignation.

"Not unless we have to," one added hopefully.

"Now, there's just one thing we need," Big John said, "and that's a man who knows Inishthorav well, a man who can lead us to where the sheep will be likely to be pastured."

There was a silence while every man looked at every other man, wondering who would reply. Big John said insistently:

"Come along, now! One man to guide us! That's all we need."

Still no one answered. Then Máirtín Thornton from

Béal Mór, at the other end of Trá Fhada, said in his drawling voice:

"Sure, don't you know well, Big John, there isn't one of us would set foot on Inishthorav? Don't you know 'tis like a geis in the old stories, that an Inishgillan man won't set his foot in friendship on that evil place?"

"Now, Máirtín, that's a hard thing to say." Big John cleared his throat and went on quickly: "But maybe someone knows Inishthorav just the same, someone that went there not in friendship, but just for a look around maybe—"

His voice trailed off. Everyone knew what he meant, all right, but it seemed that no one was willing to admit that he had sneaked ashore on Inishthorav either. It may have been too far away for passing an idle afternoon, and besides relations were too sore between us. I had not known that things were as bad as this.

"It's a difficulty," Big John said.

He turned to consult with my father and Bartley. Still I stood there in the doorway, making myself look as small as I could and wishing that I had stayed away altogether. But gradually the pounding of the blood in my ears told me quite clearly that the answer to the difficulty lay with me. I did not like it. It went against all my traditions and all my training to ask anyone to work actively against his own people, and yet I could see now that this was the best and indeed the only solution.

I left the recess and slid like a beetle along by the wall until I was pulling at my father's jersey. He turned impatiently. When he saw my face he gave me his full attention. I put my hand on his shoulder and pressed it down until his ear was close to my mouth.

"I know someone that will help us. Only you can't,

you musn't tell all the men who it is."

"I won't. Just tell us. We can keep it to ourselves."

"There's a boy here, from Inishthorav. He's up in Mamó's house now. He'll lead us to the sheep. Quiet, please, oh, please be quiet!"

He had made an exclamation at my news, and I saw that it was hard for him not to shout it out to all the company. But he kept his word, as I had known he would. He whispered for a moment in Big John's ear. Big John did not even look at me, which must have cost him an effort. Instead he just straightened his shoulders and called out:

"We'll get over that little matter of finding the sheep. It's not so important after all."

And he went on to arrange a place for the men to gather with their currachs, at the rising of the moon.

Chapter Nine

At last the men had all left the kitchen. The last fork had been taken from the pile against the outside wall, and the last man had walked lightly past the door, hurrying back to work. Their faces and their steps were full of excitement.

The doctor had not stirred. I wondered what I would do if my father were to start openly questioning me now, in his presence and in Andy's. Andy Folan never seemed to me to be really one of us, though he was my father's cousin. I think it was his carefulness in keeping his opinions to himself that I disliked. Luke did this too, in a way, but with him it was because since he represented the Government he did not want any man to feel that the Government was against him. With Andy it was a different thing. It seemed to me that he did not want to disagree with anyone for fear it might be bad for his business. There was no harm in that, you might say, but there was no good in it either, and even at that time of my life I knew that a thing must be either good or bad.

My father knew how I felt about Andy, for we had often argued about it. This may have been why he asked no questions now, but just stretched his arms wide and said:

"Out for a breath of fresh air, men! There's a plan we could try, to bring the men of Inishgillan over to Inishthorav and get them puffing at their pipes. The Inishthorav men would be laid out in rows before you could say 'cush!' to a duck."

He dropped his hand on my shoulder and we went outside together, with a word to the doctor. Big John and Bartley followed. Slowly, without any appearance of hurry, the three of them began to walk up the hill towards Mamó's house, while I walked beside my father. After a moment or two, my father said in a very quiet voice:

"Now, tell us about this boy from Inishthorav."

I told what I knew, how we had surprised him on the strand, and had learned from his own mouth that he hated the feud as much as we did and would do anything to stop it. I mentioned that King Cooney had been his father.

"A decent man," my father said. "'Tis true that he tried to make peace when he could. But 'twould take St Enda himself to make peace with the men of Inishthorav."

"They say the same about us," said Big John, "and I'm thinking that after this night's work more than one saint will be needed to make the peace between us."

"'Tis a bad business," said Bartley uneasily. "But sure, what can we do? We know they have our sheep. Isn't it a right thing to go over there and get them back? If the priest was here, wouldn't he say the same thing?"

"Maybe we should wait until Sunday and ask him what he thinks," my father suggested.

"Now, Martin," said Big John, "what on this earth will be gained by that? The priest might think of a peaceful way for getting them back, like himself going over, maybe, and preaching hellfire to them for their sins until he frightens the heart in them. That's not our way of doing things. 'Tis too roundabout. And besides that, why would we put the burden of our troubles on the priest when we can manage well enough on our own?"

When we were a hundred yards away from Mamó's cottage, Roddy appeared for an instant at her door and then he darted inside again. I wondered how Colm would feel when he heard that I was coming with three men of Inishgillan. I hurried them as much as I could, lest he might take fright after all and leave us without a guide.

As soon as we went into Mamó's kitchen I saw that he was frightened, sure enough, but he did not show any signs of running away. He stood by the mantel as if he had just sprung up off the hob, and as we came in he edged a little closer to Mamó, who was sitting in her usual chair by the hearth. I guessed that she had already made friends with him, as she did with everyone, first by giving him a good dinner and then by asking about all his aunts and cousins, at home and in America, sounding as concerned for their health and happiness as if Colm were one of our own.

I went straight to him and said:

"You want to help us to put an end to the quarrelling. The first thing is for us to get back our sheep."

I explained to him what his part in it was to be. Then I waited. We had all seen how his chin came up and his fists clenched when I had said that our men needed him to lead them to the place where the sheep would be most likely to be pastured.

"None of us knows Inishthorav," I said quickly. "And remember that if we get the sheep away without being seen there will be no fight."

"'Tis true," he said after a moment, and then he laughed sourly. "No matter what your own people do, it's hard to go against them. But I'll do it for you, of course. Isn't it for that I came?"

"Good man," said Big John. "'Tis the best way, and the only way that we can think of. We are poor people. If we were rich, we might say: 'What are a few sheep among friends?' But we can't do that, and some of our people are getting very cross."

"Faith, then, 'twill be a long time before the people of this island will be able to talk so big," said Mamó with a snort. "Not contradicting you, Big John, I'm thinking 'twill never come to pass that we'll be able to hand out sheep to every thief that comes along with his hand out."

I trembled at this, for I thought that Colm would surely take offence and refuse to help us. But he said very quietly:

"There's no one in the world able to do that. The best thing will be for me to go home to Inishthorav now, at once. I'll watch my chance when darkness falls, and I'll round up your sheep, and I'll have them all ready for you in the one place when you come."

No one answered for a moment. Then Big John asked:

"How will you do that? Surely someone will see you?"

"I'll make sure they don't see what I'm doing," Colm said. "It's like this, that when they bring over the sheep from the Grazing Island, they don't divide them out at all, some for every man. Instead of that, they hold them in common, and every man gets a share of the wool. There's one or two that won't touch it, and their share is burned. This way, they say, they're all in it together, and no man will be able to lay information on the others.

That's why those sheep are all in one flock. I have a good dog at home, and he works without barking. I'll only have to give him wind of the word and he'll help me with the sheep, after dark. They'll be running and he'll be running, and unless I'm very unlucky, no one will guess what we're doing. When you land on the White Strand, they'll be grazing in the field at the back of it. You won't even have to climb a wall. Eighteen sheep came back last night. Can you bring eighteen men with you?"

"We can and fifty."

"It would be a good thing to bring a lot of men, to manage the currachs and to look after the sheep on the way back to Inishgillan. Eighteen men only should come ashore. I'll be waiting for you. They can follow me quickly to where the sheep will be, each man can take one on his shoulders and run with it back to the currachs. I think those men needn't be as much as five minutes on the soil of Inishthorav."

"'Tis not for nothing you're King Cooney's son," Bartley said after a moment. "Anyone would think to listen to you that you had been all your life directing battles and raids."

"'Tis a fine plan, for sure," said Big John slowly. "I don't see anything at all wrong with that plan."

"Eighteen men is all that need land," my father said.

There was a long pause. Roddy and I kept very quiet. Even Mamó had no word to say, and she looked miserably from one of our faces to the other, feeling that her hospitality was not up to its usual standard when such nasty thoughts and suggestions could be flying silently around her kitchen. At last Colm said flatly:

"I know what ye're thinking, that it all depends on me whether you get back your sheep tonight. Ye're thinking

that I might get into my currach and row back to
Inishthorav, and warn all my own people that the
Inishgillan men are on the sea. Was that thought in your
mind?"

"It was," said Big John softly, "and another thought
with it, that it might be better for you to spend the night
here, nice and comfortably with Mamó, and you could
just as easily go home tomorrow when we have our sheep
safely home again. Mamó is used to strangers."

"If I don't round up the sheep for you, you'll never get
them off Inishthorav. Do you know where to look for
them, same?"

"No."

"And you might take the wrong sheep. If you were to
do that, the Inishthorav men might have the Guards
after you."

"Never!"

"They might, then, if they thought some of you could
be sent go gaol."

"It would be good for us to have a guide," said Big
John. "It will be hard to do it without a guide. I said that
from the start. I don't want to land our men on Inishthorav
and have the blood flowing in torrents. That's not the
best way, but maybe it's what we'll have to do."

"You can trust me," Colm said. "Why should I come
over here and say I wanted to help you, if I didn't mean
a word of it?"

"You might have come to find out what we were
planning," my father said.

At that moment it looked as if Colm was going to be
kept prisoner for the night, and that the men would
never trust him. It seemed to me a pity not to take
advantage of his offer to round up the sheep for us, since

this would make the whole business of recovering them very easy. All we had asked him to do was to lead us to where the sheep were most likely to be, and he had made this wonderful offer to have them all ready for us. To me he certainly looked honest. Especially when he had talked about his father, and about how the Inishthorav men had gone to the dogs since his death, he had sounded so angry that he would have had to be a practised actor indeed to have been so convincing.

I said all this to the men, and I said:

"Don't you think that there might be one honest person, same, on Inishthorav, and him the son of the King? Don't you think that even among the most out-and-out rogues and scoundrels, you might possibly find one boy that would be honest, and that would fear for his soul?"

"'Tis true, of course, 'tis possible, indeed," said Big John.

"There could be honest people on Inishthorav," said my father, and Bartley added.

"If there was an honest man, it was King Cooney, and sure, the good drop must be in this boy. Who was your mother, boy? Wasn't she a Conneeley woman from Inishmaan?"

"She was," said Colm tightly.

His face was white now, and I could imagine how hard put to it he was to swallow all those insults to his people.

My father said to me and to Roddy:

"We'll risk it. 'Tis a big risk, but 'tis worth it. There's no one to know a boy like another boy. When I was young, I remember my mother and father praising a boy from below near the slip, telling me he was a good, clean, nice boy and that he would be good company for myself. And all the time I knew him for a sneaky, slimy pysawn that you wouldn't trust as far as you'd throw him. I don't know how I knew it—something about being the same age and size with him. I knew the honest boys too, and the decent ones. So that's why I believe the two of you when you say this boy won't let us down." He said apologetically to Colm: "I'm sorry we have to talk like this. 'Tisn't decent. But we'll make up for it some day, with God's help, and we'll all be friends."

The other two said nothing, though they tried to look as if they believed we would one day be friends with the men of Inishthorav.

They all went home soon after that, refusing Mamó's offer of tea. Her feelings were very much hurt by this, and we had to stay and eat and drink with her to make up for it. But when we were finished I said immediately:

"It's time for Colm to be going home. 'Twould be a terrible thing if anyone guessed where he was."

"They'd never think of it," he said. "I have a line below in the currach, and I'll do a bit of fishing on the way home. It won't be the first time I've been out all day fishing."

We said good-bye to Mamó and started out for the strand. Colm had a huge packet of soda-bread and butter and lump of bacon, a present from Mamó to be nibbling on the way home. She came to the door to wave to us. We took him down by the lower path immediately so that he would not be seen. When she saw this she called out softly:

"You'll come back to see me, soon!"

Colm nodded to her and we dived down out of sight of the road above.

"I like her," he said. "I could spend a year and a day in her house and never feel that I wasn't welcome."

"'Tis always the way with her," Roddy said, "that she makes people feel they're doing a good turn when they eat up her food. She was the same with the doctor."

"What doctor?" Colm asked innocently.

"A doctor that stayed here once," I said quickly. "He stayed a while with Mamó, practising his Irish, and then he went off, the way they all do, and we never saw him again."

Roddy was silent. I guessed he was thinking, as I was, that it was hard to have a great secret like ours and not to be able to tell it. I could imagine how Colm would look at us with awe and admiration, when we would tell him how quickly we had seen that the doctor must not go back with the rest of the men, and how we had concealed him in Mamó's house until the whole business of the *Coriander* had been settled. But it would have been madness to tell him, and I was not in the least tempted to do it. I supposed that Roddy's remark had only been a slip of the tongue, and that he would not make that mistake again.

It was late afternoon when we saw Colm off from the Three Rocks in his currach. The sea shone in a flat calm, reflecting the red evening sky. He dipped his oars neatly and quietly, so that we could tell that he was well used to them. We watched him out a long way and then Roddy said as we turned homewards:

"'Tis a pity he doesn't come from some civilised place, that we could be friends."

"Maybe we will be, soon."

"Do you believe that? 'Twill happen when pigs fly. What we're planning tonight may be the way to get justice, but it surely isn't the way to make friends."

My spirits sank at this, for I had hoped that somehow out of this would come a new friendship with the men of Inishthorav. But now when I came to think of it clearly, I could see that Roddy was right, and that things would be almost certainly worse, if anything, than they had been before.

Suddenly I thought of something that brought me to a halt.

"Did you hear anyone say that you and I were going to be brought on the expedition tonight?"

"No, then, I did not," Roddy said after a moment's thought.

"I bet we're going to be tucked into bed," I said grimly. "I bet someone is going to say we're too young, that we can't miss a second night's sleep."

We ran like hares the rest of the way. Sure enough, I had been right. At our house, my father was finishing his tea when I arrived. I pushed open the half-door and left it standing wide while I asked him:

"Were you thinking of bringing me and Roddy with you tonight?"

"Now, Patcheen, be easy," he said soothingly. "Why should you spend the night out on the cold sea, when you could be home here in your bed?"

"Because it's more interesting," I said firmly. "I want to go with you, and see what happens."

"But you're only a boy. This is men's work."

"I'm a man since last night. Wasn't it myself and Roddy that started all this, that told ye all where the sheep are gone?"

He looked troubled, and I could see that he didn't want me to come. But I was thinking that if I were not allowed to see this evening's work, I would regret it all the days of my life. I would have lost a story to tell my children and my grandchildren, one that would be in the history of our island until the day of doom.

Behind me, the doctor had come quietly into the kitchen. My father turned to him and asked:

"What do you think, Doctor? Should we make him stay home in his bed, or should he come out with us on tonight's work?"

"Take him with you," said the doctor in his calm voice. "There will be things for him to learn. He's old enough. He can sleep until you're ready to go."

I gave him a delighted look of thanks, for I could see that my father had instantly changed his mind, so highly did he think of the doctor.

"Into bed with you, then," he said to me. "I'll call you in good time."

I went in to sleep in my father's room, after I had had a bite to eat. As I lay down, I remember thinking that the doctor really was one of us now, and that he was a very fine addition to our counsels as well as to our company.

It was night when my father awakened me. I started awake, still dreaming wildly of fairy cats sitting around a pot of potatoes, that hung over our fire on the Grazing Island. A beam of light shone into the room from the kitchen door. My father said, his hand on my shoulder:

"Come along. It's time to go now."

I shivered with a kind of horror, sorry to my heart that I had fought so hard to go. It seemed the queerest thing to get up and go out into the darkness, and hear movements of men walking all around me, as they went down to the strand. They all seemed very cheerful, and they sang little bits of songs to themselves.

Then, when I reached the turn of the road from which
I could look away off down to the sea, the moon sailed
quietly from below the horizon and lit up the whole
island. It was a full moon, dark gold at first and getting
paler with every moment. Now I could see the dark
shapes of the men hurrying along, and down on the
strand the black currachs being launched one by one so
that they lay half in and half out of the silver sea. The
moon laid a track across the sea and showed it as smooth
as a well.

"'Tis God sent us this night," my father exulted. "'Tis
made to measure for the job we have before us."

I hurried on ahead of him to look for Roddy, and soon
I found him among the crowds on the strand.

"'Tis a grand night," he said but I knew by his tone
that he was as uneasy as I was myself.

I pulled him aside where we could not be heard and
asked:

"Do you think Colm will do his part? Do you think
he'll let us down?"

"He'd never let us down," Roddy said. "It's true what
your father said, that you can tell whether a person is true
or false by the look of him."

"He didn't exactly say that."

"What's the good of being suspicious of everyone?"
Roddy said angrily. "Sure we must trust some of the
people, or we'd go raving mad."

"'Tis hard to trust an Inishthorav man. And all the
same I do trust him. I'm thinking there's some of our
own we should watch out for, though."

"Who are you talking about? Do you know
something?"

"No, no! And please be quiet. 'Tis only a feeling I have.

I don't know why it is, unless it's just the time of night, and all the talk, and where we spent last night."

"That's all imagination, then. Forget it, and we'll enjoy ourselves. 'Tisn't every night we have business like this to do."

I pretended to be busy with our currach, because I didn't want to discuss Colm any longer with Roddy. If I did, I was afraid that he would think I knew something against him, something that I had not told him. And there was nothing. I remembered every line of Colm's face, and there was nothing there to distrust. Still the heavy feeling of betrayal lay on me and I could not shake it off no matter how hard I tried.

I went in my father's boat, of course, and Roddy went with his own father. Sidecar and Bartley came with us, too, and they and my father took a pair of oars each, while I lay curled up in the stern. Through the thin canvas, I could feel the smooth sea sliding under me, as we put to sea, and then the slow curving swell that was invisible from the shore rocked us gently up and down.

Simon and Stephen Conneeley, the twins that lived near the slip, headed out the fastest for Inishthorav. Soon we were like a flight of wild geese, with the twins' currach in front and the rest of us spread out in a huge V behind it. When they saw this, the twins slowed down a little and suited their pace to ours. If anyone showed signs of going faster, they pulled on ahead too, for they wanted above all things to lead every party.

During the first half-hour we had one song after another to pass the time. I wished very much that Luke was with us, for Luke had a fine voice and he knew all the old fighting songs that would make your blood boil inside you. But Luke was not there, of course, because of being a Government official. He had come down to the slip to watch the currachs go, but he had turned home as soon as we began putting to sea. I thought then that I must point this out to Roddy, who was going to be the postmaster some day, and ask him how he would like to have his wings clipped in this way. I certainly knew that it would not suit me at all, though naturally there would be times when it would save a lot of trouble.

In half an hour, Big John Moran put a stop to the singing. After that we went like a fleet of ghosts. Though there was no need for it yet, the men dipped and lifted their oars with as little splash as possible, practising for when we would be near Inishthorav. The night air was cold, and the moon no longer looked friendly. It was too far away and too pale.

For most of the journey, we could see the black back of Inishthorav away off in front of us. As we came nearer to it, tiny lights, no bigger than the head of a pin, showed here and there. The nearer we came, the bigger and yellower these became, and then they began to go out, one by one. I had a fine view of this, but the men at the oars had their backs to it and they rarely turned their heads to look. It was not necessary, indeed, for they could have found any piece of land in those waters blindfold.

"Were you never in Inishthorav at all?" I asked my father, who was sitting nearest to me.

"I was, faith," he said. "'Twas at a wedding the last time I was there."

"Are some of the Inishthorav people married in with our people, then?"

"They are, to be sure. Thirty years ago, there was great coming and going between Inishgillan and Inishthorav.

They'd come over to us for a day and we'd go to them. We'd have sports and dancing and singing till morning. Ay, 'twas like that until about thirty years ago."

"Thirty-two years next St John's Day," said Bartley's voice behind him.

"And what happened?" I asked after a moment, when neither of them spoke again. "I thought there was always bad blood between us."

"'Twas this wedding," said my father after a pause. "'Twas a bad business, there's no denying. Manus Griffin's daughter Peggy was marrying into Inishthorav—"

"I never knew he had a daughter Peggy," I said in astonishment.

"She was his youngest girl, a fine one too, red hair and full of life and talk, not a bit like Nora. She wasn't twenty, nor nineteen, at the time, a grand upstanding girl. She married Mark Regan from Inishthorav and of course we all went over for the wedding. We had no fault to find with what they gave us, the newest of food and the oldest of drink, as the old stories say. We had a look at where Peggy was going to live, and we had no fault with that either. 'Twas a fine house with no less than four rooms in it and a fine hearth with lovely hobs and a clock wagging its tail on the wall. Any girl would be glad to go into it."

"And what happened?" I asked again.

"Everything was fine at first, and then out in the evening, Mark Regan's sister said that Peggy was going into a better house than herself would ever see. We thought first that 'twas praising her own house she was, and she had a right to do that for 'twas a fine house. But she said it again, and Nora's husband Tom, God rest him, asked what did she mean. Faulting the size of Peggy's dowry she was, as it turned out, for of course she would get the most of that to bring with her when she'd be married, and I suppose she was thinking that 'twould only bring her into a small place.

"Tom rose up and said we'd all be going home to Inishgillan, and he'd take his sister-in-law with him if they didn't mind, since that was the class of talk that they had about her, and that she'd be disrespected if we left her there. But not a stir of Peggy would come with us. Her father told her to come, that she was within her rights, and he'd tell the priest what happened, and God nor man wouldn't expect her to stay with people that had insulted her and all belonging to her. But she wouldn't leave Mark Regan, she said, for gold nor silver, nor for all the wagging tongues in the western hemisphere. So we rose up, every man of us—I was only young at the time and no one asked my opinion—and we went home, and for most of us that was the last time we set foot in Inishthorav."

"Was that the beginning of all the crossness between our people and the people of Inishthorav?"

"It was, I suppose. There was a great falling-out once before, about a hundred years ago. My grandfather knew the ins and outs of that, though he wasn't any way concerned in it. It was patched up and no one thought such a thing would ever happen again until the falling-out over Peggy's dowry. After that, every Inishgillan man went out of his way to down every Inishthorav man, and sure, 'twasn't long until the new insults covered the old ones, and Peggy was forgotten."

"Did she ever come back to Inishgillan?"

"Never once. She never laid eyes on Manus from that day to this. Her mother was under the sod with a few years, before the wedding. 'Tis a sad story, indeed, and 'tis a pity it ever happened. I'd like to see the end of such crossness between neighbours."

"Why didn't her father go over to Inishthorav to see her?" I insisted. "Why didn't he ever talk about her? 'Tis a mighty queer thing when I didn't even know he had a daughter except Nora."

"'Tis a queer thing when the young will start telling the old what they should do," said Bartley.

I wished I had my father alone, for he would have talked more freely then. Bartley was a great man for keeping the young in their place, which may have been one reason why all of his sons had gone off to Portland and left him alone. My father said:

"It was Peggy's place to visit her father, and she never came. 'Twas hard on her too, I'm thinking, but the story goes that she felt bound to go with her husband and her husband's people, and that's what a good wife should do, for sure and certain. Four sons and two daughters she had, if we heard the truth. Thirty-two years is a long time, and Manus Griffin is not getting younger. 'Tis doubtful if she'll ever see him in this life, for by the looks of things, it's not getting fonder of each other we are."

I thought this a terribly sad story, and I blamed the Inishgillan men for what had happened as much as the men of Inishthorav. Young people have an easy way out of everything, and it seemed to me that our people should have taken no notice of what Mark Regan's sister had said. She was probably jealous of Peggy for being such a good-looking girl and for getting into such a good house. Above all I pitied old Manus, for he was a sociable man, as I could see from his friendship with the doctor, and it must have hurt him to have one of his family so near and yet not able to drop in on a Sunday for a chat and a gossip.

We were silent then, for we were coming near to Inishthorav. Close to, it looked huge and black and frightening in the dark. Not a light showed anywhere now, not the smallest spark to give a sign that the island was inhabited at all.

Big John moved up near the twins, and spoke to them. I guessed that he was explaining that we could no longer travel in V formation. I knew that there was to be nothing haphazard about our landing. It was to be disciplined, and following a plan that had been well talked over.

Giving his orders in a loud whisper, Big John got all the currachs lined up about five hundred yards off the shore. A few strokes of the oars and they were a hundred yards nearer, still in line. We were in the next boat to Big John, and the twins were to the other side of us. On an order from Big John the oars dipped softly again and we were nearer in and riding the little swell. The pale moon shone thinly down on the White Strand, a long curve of silver with a great mass of black shadow at one end of it. Then, in a voice that will never leave my ears until the day I die, Big John said aloud:

"T'anam 'on diabhal! The whole population is down to meet us!"

Every boat rocked, as every man turned on the thwarts to peer towards the island. Then the Inishthorav men knew that we had seen them. The dark mass moved and opened out as the men spread along the beach, running like thirsty cattle down to the water's edge. A voice floated over to us, vibrating on the still air:

"You're coming on a visit at a queer time of the night!

'Tisn't the time for honest visitors!"

"Come closer, men, come closer!" another voice invited us derisively. "A few yards more, just a small bit more!"

"We'll send every one of your currachs to the bottom of the sea," another voice called out, in real anger this time and not merely jeering.

"I know you, Mike Rua!" Tomás Rua shouted from his currach.

I could hear it splashing about as he pranced on the thwart with rage. Big John said:

"Easy, Tomás, easy! There's no good in wrecking yourself. They've got the better of us this time."

I could hear the despair and humiliation in his voice, and it hurt me through and through. Mike Rua called out again:

"Land your army, you thieving cowards! Come on and fight it out with us. The winners can have the sheep. And they can have the doctor too!"

We could see now that every man on the strand carried a fork or a harpoon or a scythe. It would have been madness indeed to have accepted their invitation, not only for our own sake, but because every one of our currachs would have been sent to the bottom of the sea. Big John said after a moment:

"There's nothing to be done here, men. Home to Inishgillan. That's all we can do."

And the whole fleet turned around and set out for home.

Chapter Ten

Hardly a word was spoken on the way home, neither in our boat nor in any of the others. One and all, the men were in such a fury that they seemed not to be able to use their tongues. Sometimes my father or Bartley MacDonagh would begin to say something, but after a word or two, they would stop, almost as if they had forgotten what they had intended to say.

I lay very low in the currach, hoping that neither of them would speak to me. For me that was the longest journey in the world, and the worst of it was that I knew that even when we would land, the journey would seem to go on and on for ever. A great pain filled my chest as if a hand in there were moving around my heart, and squeezing it in and out. One name kept hammering over and over in my brain until I thought it would leave me silly for life. Colm, Colm Cooney. He had looked so honest. I had urged the men to trust him. He had promised us his help, all without asking, and then he had let us walk into a trap that would have lost us our boats and humiliated us before all the islands of Galway for a year and a day.

I could imagine how he must have landed at

Inishthorav and gone straight to the house of the man that sent him to us, saying:

"It was very easy. I met two silly boys on the strand. They were suspicious at first but I was able to fool them. They brought three men to see me, and I promised that I would gather up the sheep and have them waiting. Imagine what fools they must be to believe that I would play a trick like that on the men of my own island!"

Sweat broke out all over me as I imagined how he would have said then:

"It's not sheep I'll have waiting for them!"

The worst part of that journey was our landing at the slip. The women were all there to welcome us, and they had got sods of turf and dipped them in paraffin oil and lighted them, and they had them stuck on hay-forks where they flared like torches in the still air. Away out at sea, we could hear them singing, already celebrating our victory, so sure were they that we had the currachs loaded with sheep. As we came close in I could hear old Mamó's voice raised in a song that she used to teach us at school: "The cow with one horn." This song tells of a man's longing to own a cow with one horn, and later in the same song he says that he would rather than a shilling to see his own sheep come to the door in the morning or in the evening; the sheep would give milk and bear a lamb, and also provide a nice little jacket for his son. It was for the piece about the sheep that Mamó was singing this song. As soon as she had finished it she began on another song about sheep:

"I wish I had the shepherd's pet."

The men were very patient. No one shouted to the women to be quiet. The singing died away as soon as the first currach landed, and then we heard all of the women give sharp little cries of distress. Mamó came running over to our boat.

"He was a liar after all, that boy. And he was old enough to know better. Small boys do be liars, because they know no better, but that boy was nearly a man, and 'tis a bad thing to be a liar at his time of life."

She said it as if he were suffering from some disease which was incurable because of his age. Then, in the light of her flaming sod of turf, she saw my distressed face and she said kindly:

"Sure, anyone could make a mistake about a person, Patcheen. There's liars and traitors walking the roads of every country in the great world. You couldn't pass through life without coming up against at least one of them. May all your bad luck go with him, the little caffler. If I could catch him, I'm telling you I'd give him Mary's Spinning Wheel."

She meant it consolingly, but all this abuse of Colm only made me feel worse. I was glad when my father answered her instead of me:

"'Tis true that we were nicely fooled. I haven't felt like that since I was a young lad. They invited us to land and fight it out, but I'm thinking they knew we wouldn't do that. God help us, we could never do the like of that."

"Never, never," said all the men standing around.

A cold, searching wind was fluttering up and down the strand. It was about two o'clock in the morning, the time when the old people die, the time when life is at its weakest. The moon was gone, but we had plenty of light from the torches. The sea seemed callously cold when we waded into it to bring our currachs ashore. It shone smooth and hard, like polished metal. The pebbles at its edge rattled under each wave, with a dull, lonesome sound that made me want to cry. Then, one by one, quite silently, the women began to move up the hill from the slip, carrying their torches. One by one the lights went out as each woman went into her own house. We followed them up the road in a crowd. My father said, with an effort to be cheerful:

"We'll have another day. 'Tisn't as easy as all that to get the better of us."

"'Tis true for you," said all the men uneasily, and one could tell that they were at a loss to imagine what could be done next.

My mother had been at the strand, and she had tea ready for us when we got in home. The fire was blazing up, the little lamp was lighted in front of the holy picture, and the big brassy lamp with the globe was on the kitchen table. All of these lights made the china on the dresser glow and sparkle, and put a rosy tint on the whitewashed walls, and on the brown teapot that stood on the table. I felt warmer just from the sight of it, and especially of my settle bed ready waiting for me. A thought was buzzing around in my head, like a summer bee that has got between the geraniums and the window-pane and can't get out again. But I could not attend to it now. After I had eaten, I rolled into bed and in a few minutes I was fast asleep, even with the lamp burning and my father and mother talking to each other in low voices at the kitchen table.

My head was a lot clearer when I awoke next morning. It was very early. Not even my mother was stirring. I got up and laid a few sods of turf on the hot ashes of last night's fire, to get them used to the idea of burning. Then I put on some clothes and went out into the sharp air. The hens were roosting in soft heaps on the cart that was restingon its shafts in the shed. They had a house of their own, but for some reason they preferred the cart shed. One of them flopped to the ground when she saw me, and then strolled slowly into the back of the shed. A few minutes later, as I was going down the hill to Roddy's house, I heard her begin on her tune: "Gug-gug-gug-gug-gawk! Gug-gug-gug-gug-gawk!" It was like the voice of the morning itself. In a few minutes every hen on the island would have heard it, and would be reminded to lay an egg herself and have something to glory about. Always when I heard them on a fine sunny morning like this, I remembered what Mamó had told us at school, that the hen shouts when she lays an egg:

"I laid an egg, an egg, an egg and still I'm going BARE-foot."

And the cock replies:

"I bought you boots and boots and boots and still you won't WEAR them!"

The children always call an egg "Gug", because it seems that that is what the hen herself calls it, and who should know better?

Roddy's house door was still shut, but I went to his window and peered in through the glass. He was lying in bed, and as I watched him he stretched and yawned and opened his eyes. I tapped on the glass with my nails and he sprang up, fully awake, and came across to look out at me, like a fish in a jam jar. I jerked my arm at him, to signal him to come outside, and then I went to sit on the low wall in front of his house.

It seemed a long time before he came, but he was worth waiting for, because he had thought of bringing a piece of soda-bread for each of us. We walked down the road, away from the houses. I waited until we were passing the flat flagstones, where we have the dances, before I spoke. I could not look at him as I asked the question that had been burning me unknown to myself last night, and that had been falling off my tongue since I had wakened up:

"When you were alone with Colm Cooney yesterday, did you tell him all about the doctor?"

"I did not! On my solemn oath, I never said a single word—"

"I heard you say a single world. And you said it as if you had already told him every word of the doctor's story. 'She was the same with the doctor,' you said, as if Colm would know at once who you were talking about."

"If you have such a good memory, maybe you'll remember that he asked: 'What doctor?' as if he had never seen a doctor in his life."

"That might be because you had warned him to say nothing about it."

"And why would I do such a thing? Do you take me for an out-and-out fool? 'Tis you that trusted him, not me."

"You did too. You said he looked honest."

"So he does. That's what makes it so easy for him to fool the people."

"And you never told him that we have the doctor off the *Coriander* here, safe and sound, working for us? You never told him that?"

"Sorro' word. Nor I didn't mention the *Coriander* either. Don't I know as well as yourself what is fitting to tell to a stranger."

"Then why did the men of Inishthorav call out to us that the winners of the fight could have the sheep, and the doctor as well?"

"They said that?"

"Didn't you hear them?"

"I don't know. They said that word, for sure, but last night I couldn't think. I could only see them all there, like pookas, like a nightmare—they said whoever would win could have the sheep and the doctor?"

"That's what I heard."

Still walking down towards the slip, we began to work out what this had meant. The cool, clean, morning air swept the cobwebs out of our brains, I suppose, for all at once we realised what had happened.

It came to us at the same moment. Roddy said:

"Pat, we should put our two heads up for sale. Do you know what happened last night?"

"Colm is honest. It wasn't Colm at all."

"No, and another thing: it wasn't you nor I that was the cause of last night's disaster."

"That's a good thought, so it is. I was thinking we'd never hear the last of it. After we persuading the men to trust Colm. The people won't be so uncivil to us now. But I'm heart-sorry, all the same," I said. "'Tis nearly as bad as if it was Colm."

"It may be nearly as bad, but the doctor didn't come to us saying he wanted to help us, the way Colm did. We captured him, the way you would capture a man in battle, and we held him prisoner against his will. That is enough to turn a man against you for ever. We let Colm go. We just gave him a good dinner and let him go home. The doctor must have been plotting and scheming unknown to us, for weeks and months, how to get away from us."

It hurt me to hear him say this, though I knew it must be true. All the time, when the doctor and I had been going around together, visiting the sick people, and while he had been telling me so many things that my head was bursting with new knowledge, all that time he had been hating me and all my people. It must have been so, or else he would not have put us in danger of our lives, as well as of the loss of our boats. If we had landed last night on the White Strand of Inishthorav, who knows but that a man might have been killed with a scythe, and another drowned? God save us all, I thought, there's no island man born would send his worst enemy into a trap like that.

"He must have sent a message on the telegraph," Roddy was saying. "He knows how to work it, for I heard him say as much to Luke one day. He didn't tell him straight. He just dropped it out, that when he was on the *Coriander* he learned all about her navigation and radio and everything else."

"Luke should have noticed that. We could have kept a watch on him if we had known it."

"Sure, Luke trusts him like one of his own. And didn't I hear him myself and I never thought of it, that he'd use the telegraph to make his escape. He couldn't have done that either, until lately. Luke wouldn't leave his own mother, if she was alive, within a yard of the telegraph. But with all the excitement I suppose he got careless and left him alone with it. A few minutes would be enough. You'd need experience of the world to be able to do this kind of thing right."

"It seems so. And now we'll have to tell what we know, so that the same thing won't happen again."

"Isn't the harm done now?" Roddy pointed out. "Our only chance of keeping the doctor was that the whole world would think him drowned. We were calling the

Inishthorav men all sorts of names for stealing a few sheep, and isn't it a lot worse to steal a Christian than a sheep? I'm thinking that this will be the beginning of great misfortune for Inishgillan."

I was thinking the same thing and I was not a bit pleased with him for agreeing with me. He was always more gloomy than I was. If we went fishing, he always prophesied that we would catch nothing. If I were as sure as he appeared to be, I'd stay at home altogether. It never occurred to him to stay at home: he would go, and he would expect nothing. If he were proved wrong, he would be glad at having cheated his fate. If he were proved right, he would enjoy a special kind of sour satisfaction.

"Don't salute the devil until he salutes you," I said.

At the slip we looked across at the twin Conneeleys' house. A thread of smoke was going up from the chimney but the door was not yet open. Every door that we had passed on the way down the hill was firmly shut, and you could tell by the look of the houses that the people in them were not yet stirring.

And yet, out on the pale-grey sea there was a single currach. We went down to the end of the slip to see whose it was. The man in it had his back to us, for he was rowing towards the shore Then we saw him glance once over his shoulder. He gave a few more strong pulls on his oars, until he was only twenty yards away from us. We could see a fringe of red hair below his woollen cap. With two quick jerks of one oar, he brought the currach around, and we were staring into the face of a green-eyed stranger.

"That's an Inishthorav boat," said Roddy in a low voice.

The man must have had fox's ears, for he answered.

"'Tis an Inishthorav boat, to be sure, and an Inishthorav man inside in it, as who has a better right." He swept off his cap and bowed to us mockingly. "Michael Sayers, at your service. They do call me Mike Rua. I have a message for you, from the men of Inishthorav."

We made no reply, but stood there stiff with terror. It was a completely unreasonable terror, for this man clearly meant us no personal harm. But we had been brought up with such a poor opinion of the Inishthorav men that it would hardly have surprised us if he had rushed ashore and slaughtered us with the blade of an oar. He did not expect a reply, it seemed, for he went on directly to give his message:

"You can tell the Inishgillan men that we are heartily thankful to them, for the fine sheep they have been sending us this while back but we won't be wanting any more now for a while. We'll put our own sheep to graze on the Grazing Island from this on, but we'll be kind of nervous about them, so we'll always leave a few men with them, to guard them, in case any thief might come and take them away. And you can tell the Inishgillan men another thing that they'll maybe find very interesting, that the Guards will be out from Galway this very day to take the doctor out of his captivity, and to take one-half of ye away to gaol!"

He burst into a great roar of laughter at the shocked look on our faces. Then he turned his currach quickly and set out for home, pulling with long easy strokes and grinning back at us as he went.

When we turned away from the slip, we saw that Simon Conneeley was standing only a yard or two away. His brother was on his way down from the house. I thought that Simon would start questioning me, but he just looked at me as if he didn't see me at all. Then his eyes travelled after the man in the currach and back to me again, and I think I have never seen such wild black rage in the eyes of any man before or since then. It was a sample of what was before us, I supposed, and I was glad that I did not have to speak to him. I seized Roddy by the arm and swung him around, and we ran back together, by the way that we had come.

The houses were all humming now. The ducks and hens were pecking in clusters at their breakfast, the children were running in and out with armfuls of turf and cans of water, the men were smoking their first pipes while they tackled the donkeys to the carts or selected their tools for the morning's work. Big John did not have to go out to work so early, being a pensioner. We found him sitting at the head of the table in his own kitchen, just lifting his second mug of tea for a drink. He put it down carefully when he saw our faces. When he had heard what we had come to tell him, he got up and came outside the door. He walked between us to our house, and to Tomás Rua's, and to Bartley's house, and then back to Luke's. In each of those houses we told our story, and in each the man of the house put down what he was doing and came with us. At our house, the door of the doctor's room had been shut, and I had beckoned my father outside before speaking.

Once the men that we had summoned were congregated in Luke's kitchen, one by one all the men of the island began to gather in. It is hard to say how word travels around so fast, but it does travel, faster than summer dust, faster than a fairy wind. There they were, rumbling with talk, their pipes puffing and gurgling, and no man listening to anyone but himself. I did not go into Luke's house at all.

"We have something to do, quickly," I said to Roddy.

I knew we had a little time, for I had seen the twin Conneeleys at Luke's house, standing silently shoulder to shoulder, against the back wall. A few steps away from Luke's door, Roddy held my arm and said:

"Are you thinking—what I'm thinking?"

"There's no time to waste in talk," I said, shaking myself free.

I did not want to look at him. I began to run and the stones of the road seemed to burn my bare feet. My knees felt sore and stiff, as if I hadn't run for a week, because I was trying to force them to take steps that would need seven-league boots. Roddy ran beside me. He did not repeat his question, but after a moment I said, with my eyes on the road:

"The doctor's life is in danger. I'd swear that Simon has thought of killing him. If the doctor is not here, who can prove that he ever was here? What Simon thinks now, Stephen thinks in ten minutes' time. When the two of them think the same thing, they do the same thing."

At our house, by the mercy of God my mother had gone out to the shed to look at a new litter of pigs that our sow had had a few days before. She had laid the doctor's breakfast on the table and just as we ran into the kitchen he was coming out of his room door.

He moved forward quietly, lifting his eyebrows a little, thinking, I suppose, that he knew why we looked so agitated.

"Good morning to you both," he said calmly, sitting down at the table. "Did you sleep well? Ah, yes, I remember that you were not anxious for sleep. You wanted to go out in the currach with your father. Did you learn anything?"

"Put that egg and the bread in your pocket. You must come with us and hide."

"No, no. I'm finished with hiding. That's all over now."

"Come with us for the love of God!"

"Is someone sick?" the doctor asked sharply.

"No, no. It's not that."

"Then I'll begin my breakfast if you please."

In desperation I saw that there was no hope of moving him unless we explained his danger exactly. I sat at the table and breathed in and out several times before I could find the right words. The doctor took the top off his egg and buttered a slice of bread. I said to Roddy:

"Go out and keep watch, and if you see either of the twins coming, run in at once and tell us."

Roddy did as I told him. Then I turned to the doctor:

"Your life is in danger. An Inishthorav man told us the Guards are coming to arrest whoever kept you here against your will. Simon Conneeley heard him. Simon and Stephen always want to be out in front of everything. Myself and Roddy could see what he was thinking of—oh, we saw as well as if there was a window in his brain! He was thinking of murder, and that the Guards might search and search and never find you, and then they'd think that the Inishthorav men had brought them out to make fools of them, and they'd have a grudge against them for ever and a day. But the Inishgillan men would thank Simon for saving them, and from this day out himself and Stephen would be treated like heroes."

"Would the Inishgillan men thank Simon?" the doctor asked, very softly, his eyes on my face.

"They'd be shamed and sorry for the rest of their lives. Don't you know that well? They think of you like one of their own. Come with us, and we'll hide you. We know a place—"

"How do I know you won't lead me to my death?"

"Because you saw me, how I learned from yourself to put life in people."

He stared at me flatly. He did not seem to be afraid, but rather calculating how best he could manage to make his life last longer. One thing was clear, that he did not know whether or not to trust me. His problem was settled by Roddy running into the kitchen. His face was a greenish-white.

"He's coming," he said hoarsely, "up by the very edge of the road, walking quietly on the grass."

"Out by the back way," I said.

Roddy ran to open the back door. I prayed that my mother would not see us. There was no time to tell her what had happened, and I feared that she would direct Simon after us. But the door of the pig-house faced away from the house and she did not come out.

The doctor was moving as fast as either of us now, making no more objections and clearly having decided that this was no time for questions. Behind our house, a grassy, narrow boreen led between briar-grown stone walls to a wild field that was never tilled. It was too rocky, even for Inishgillan which has more than a decent share of rocks in every field. It did very well for grazing our goats. I think they found the rocks interesting, for climbing.

We got over the wall into this field, and I felt more at ease there. The rocks would make cover for us as we crossed the field. I hoped that Simon would stay some time in our kitchen, waiting for the doctor to come in. His breakfast laid out on the table would make it look as if he would be in at any moment, for he had not taken my advice about putting it in his pocket.

On the other hand, it might occur to Simon that the doctor had abandoned his breakfast in a hurry and fled. But Simon's brain was slow, and it would take him some time to work it out.

Behind one of the rocks, I made the others lie low and I looked back. It was all quiet down there, the very picture of peace, with the slow smoke rising from the chimney and the hens stepping slowly about in the thick green grass. Then I saw my mother come around from the pig-house and go towards the kitchen door. I hustled the other two on, for she would surely hold Simon in talk for a minute or two, and this would be long enough for us to get the doctor over the loose stone wall at the top of the field.

Beyond the wall, we stopped for long enough to look through the holes between the stones, down towards our house. There came Simon, walking slowly and looking even at this distance, frightening. It was something about the short, heavy steps that he took, that gave this effect, like a man tracking a huge wild animal. We waited only while he took the first step towards the lane by which we had come. Under my breath I said:

"Run, now, if you ever ran in your life!"

I followed my own advice, and went plunging down the hill. Below us were the Three Rocks that had sent us the *Coriander*, which had seemed such a blessing at the time. Now I wished I had never laid an eye on her, that I would have to depend all my born days on the work of my own hands, that we had never piled up her treasure in our caves.

With this thought came the solution to the problem that had been tormenting me ever since we had left our house: where on all of our island were we to hide the doctor and keep him safe? This time there would be no question of taking him to Mamó's house. Simon meant murder. An old woman could never defend him, and besides that, the terror of it all might be the death of her. I thought of Manus Griffin's house, and the shed with the loom where he might be safe for a while behind the bales of cloth. But Simon would think of looking for him there, since he knew that Manus and the doctor were friends.

Now I knew that the only safe place for him was in one of the secret caves at the outermost tip of the island. We had reached the track that ran along the top of the shore. Roddy and the doctor turned towards the slip.

"The other way," I said sharply.

"My leg is getting sore," the doctor said.

"By heaven," said I, "if you don't want a mighty sore throat, you'd better put that leg under your arm and run."

He ran, but he limped. My heart was sorry for him, but I would not think of it. I ran beside Roddy.

"To the caves we'll take him," I panted into his ear. "If we don't, he's a dead man."

"To the caves! You can't do that! No outside man has ever seen the caves."

"There's one going to see them now."

"Is it the only place?"

"It's the only place where Simon will never look. He won't believe that we would ever let a stranger see them."

"I'd rather death than for him to see them!"

"Death for yourself, maybe, but would you rather death for the doctor?"

"'Tis a terrible responsibility to let him see them."

"Either he sees the caves or he'll see God in five minutes' time. I would die ten times myself before I would let him die."

I was no longer whispering. In front of us the doctor stopped and said:

"What is it? What are your arguing about?"

"Run! Run!"

He turned and ran, and I ran beside him. I could not look at him as I said:

"We trusted you before and you betrayed us. For all that we'll have to trust you again. Or maybe it's not that at all but that we must throw away all we have in this world to save a man's life."

He made no answer, and Roddy said not another word either. We all needed our breath now for the last part of that terrible flight. It still comes back to me in my dreams, especially on stormy nights when the howling winds make the whole house shudder and disturb everyone's sleep. Then I feel again the dragging weakness of the doctor as we helped him over the smoothly-worn rocks, over the deep fissures and the little tumbling river that separated the end of the path from the mouth of the first cave. That cave opened onto a tiny beach of shingle which was covered at the spring tides. The opening faced out to sea, and since one side of it jutted out further than the other a stranger in a boat would have thought that the cliff's face was whole.

Light came in through the cave's mouth and through a hole high on the front wall, almost like a window. We moved into the shadows. The doctor said:

"It's like Aladdin's cave." He paused while he looked around at the things that were stowed against every wall and on almost every inch of the floor. "Did you take the whole *Coriander* asunder and bring the pieces in here?"

"Have you good nerves?" I asked. "You're not safe yet."

"What do you want me to do?"

"I'll show you."

I led him through a narrow opening into the second cave. This was where lighter things were stored, things that were not so bulky. It was a fine dry cave, suitable for sacks of flour and meal, whenever we were lucky enough to have them. It was here that the *Coriander's* bunks were stored. Tomás Rua had had charge of them. He had roped them together, two and two, so that each pair of bunks was like a long flat box.

"Between a pair of those bunks, no one will ever find you," I said.

Then I wished I had not put it in that way. He looked at me for a long moment before he said:

"Very well. I think you wish me no harm. But if I am found, will it be the end of me?"

"You can be saying your prayers inside in the bunk," said Roddy, and he seemed to mean it kindly.

We took the ropes off a pair of bunks, and the doctor lay down on one of them. Then we put the other one on top like a lid and roped them up again, imitating Tomás Rua's knots as nearly as possible. We piled several other pairs of bunks on top of him. I knelt on the floor beside him and said, through a chink between the bunks:

"Have you enough air?"

"Yes. I wish the other bunks didn't have to be on top of me."

"It can't be helped. He'd notice if he were to come in that one pair was out on the floor alone. Are you afraid?"

"Of course I'm afraid." Then to my astonishment and delight I heard him give a little chuckle. "I never thought I'd lie in a *Coriander* bunk again."

"We'll be back to let you out, the first moment we can," I said.

Roddy was waiting for me outside in the sunlight. His face was white.

"I couldn't stand it," he said. "I had to come out. How long will he have to stay in there?"

"Until the Guards come."

"God help us, 'tis like a coffin."

I could not find any answer to this. It seemed to knock all the air out of my lungs. After a long pause I said:

"We'll go back now and find out what has been happening in the last hour."

We did not speak a single word all the way back from that secret place, nor while we climbed up from the lower path onto the road near Mamó's house, and walked down to Big John's. There, though his kitchen was full to the doors, we walked into a silence as deep as our own.

Chapter Eleven

No one took any notice of us. We stayed by the door and looked around us. It seemed as if the men were all looking down at their feet, shifting a little from one to the other so that it was almost like watching a dance. Big John was standing with his back to the fire. He was the tallest man there, and he was able to let his eyes travel over them all, one by one. Standing beside him, Bartley MacDonagh looked very uneasy. So did my father, but he looked more angry than Bartley, who seemed to be trying to make peace.

"Now, men," Bartley said after a minute or two, "you know Big John is right. There's only one thing to be done, and that's what he said."

Sidecar said sharply:

"We don't like the Guards on Inishgillan, nor never did. You should hear the things they do to the poor people in Aran—turning them out of the public houses at eleven o'clock at night—that class of thing. We won't have them put foot on Inishgillan while I'm alive to defend it."

Several of Sidecar's friends muttered at this, and it seemed that they agreed with him. Bartley said:

"What Big John told you is what God Himself would tell you, or the priest if he were here."

"I'm not so sure of that. A man has a right to defend his own, as no one knows better than Big John. Would he say that we stole the *Coriander* and that we ought to give it back? Would he lead the Guards to the caves, where no man but an Inishgillan man has ever set foot, and show them all the lovely things?"

Roddy and I glanced at each other sideways. Bartley said hotly:

"He would not. The *Coriander* was wrack."

"I wouldn't trust him! I wouldn't trust an inch of him! Didn't he send away the lovely suits that I do be dreaming of every night since? The trouble with Big John is that he learned too many foreign notions when he was away on the ships and in the far countries."

"Sidecar, you're talking like a pagan!"

"I'm talking like an Inishgillan man born and bred. How do we know how many men the Guards will want to take away? Are we all to walk like—like *sheep*, onto their boat, the way the Inishthorav men took our sheep off the Grazing Island? The Galwaymen don't love the islandmen. Don't you know in your heart and soul that if they got us in there in that big city, we'd be lost and bewildered, and they'd have a rope around our necks and have us strung as high as they strung Lynch the day long ago—"

"They would not!"

"'Tis their reputation, faith," said Sidecar. "And why should we put ourselves into the power of people with a name like that?"

Big John said quietly:

"But you don't believe we can keep the doctor now?"

"He can go out in a currach and get into the Guards' boat, and go away with them, like any visitor. He's a decent man. There's no way out of that. We know the doctor must go."

I saw Stephen Conneeley jerk his chin up at this, enjoying in advance the praise that he and his brother would get later. Then while I watched him, he began to move slowly towards the door. Terror seized me, at the thought of what they were planning. Simon's and Stephen's heads together made up almost as much sense as one ordinary man. If they were to meet now, they might by some terrible chance work out where the doctor was hiding. I wished that I could stop the meeting with one shout, but I was afraid. If I were to tell where the doctor was and say that he must be protected from the twins, how did I know but that one of these men, or even Sidecar himself, might think that Simon and Stephen had the right idea?

Big John was saying, quietly and reasonably:

"You say the doctor must go. Surely he'll tell the Guards, what they know already from the Inishthorav men, that we kept him here a prisoner against his will for the most of six months. While there's law and order in Ireland, the Government won't stand for that. They won't just warn the doctor to stay on dry land in future. They'll be out with guns and drums to arrest somebody. That's the way with all governments, and it's no good going against it."

"Faith, then, there's many a man here present in this room that would go against it, same as their ancestors went against Cromwell the day long ago. And you're forgetting something."

"What am I forgetting?"

"That when we had no doctor, we said, 'no doctor, no rates.' I'd swear 'twas in every man's mind when the doctor came from heaven to us, that if 'twas ever discovered that we had him here we'd owe a pile of rates to the Government. Well, we're willing to pay the rates now, every penny. When the Government sees that, it won't mind about the doctor."

"Do you mean you think the doctor will be left here?" Big John asked in a flat voice.

"Ara, no. How could I believe that? What I'm saying is that 'twill soften them a bit and they won't be so inclined to bother us about the six months we had him here without leave."

"They won't be softened at all," Big John said positively. "I'll say now what I said before, that the best of our play is to give up the doctor, and for some of us to agree to go with the Guards when they come. Inside in Galway, whoever goes with the Guards will have to explain why we kept the doctor, and make such a case for a doctor on Inishgillan that they'll do all they can from this out to send us one."

"If it's true for themselves, they did all they could in that direction long ago," Sidecar said. A cunning look came over his face and suddenly he pointed his finger at Big John. "And who would be the best man to go with the Guards? Who is the leader of the people? Yourself, of course!"

Big John raised his eyebrows at this, and looked at Sidecar with amusement.

"I'm always ready to practise what I preach," he said. "I'm never afraid of saying what I think, any place in the world. Did you think yourself would be our best representative, maybe? You're welcome to come along.

They'll never be satisfied to take only one."

Sidecar was silent. My father said quietly:

"I'll go with you, John. It can't be Luke, because of the post office. The boy can look after the place if I'm away for a while."

No one had mentioned gaol, but that was what was in their minds, as we all knew. I felt all my courage trickle away, at the thought of my father and Big John being in gaol. And yet I knew from the history book and from the old stories that it sometimes does happen that an honest man must go to gaol or even to his death, for the good of all.

Big John glanced once at my father and said:

"Thanks, Martin. Now, let everyone listen to me carefully. There's not a word to be said about the *Coriander* while the Guards are on the island, not a single word. The Inishthorav men don't know what happened to her. The doctor himself doesn't know what happened to her. The last thing we did with her, he was over in Manus Griffin's place talking about the great Amazon River. If no one tells, no one will know."

All the men muttered that they would never tell. Big John went on:

"There will be a hard trial of us, when the doctor walks on to the Guards' boat and goes away with them. We were foolish, I suppose, to get so fond of him. He was like one of our own. We told him every bit of our business except one thing only, that was never told to a soul yet, but to Inishgillan men only. 'Twas well we never told him where the caves are, for he would surely tell the Guards about them in revenge for being kept prisoner—"

Suddenly I was shouting:

"He would not! He would never do the like of that! He only wanted to get away!"

"Maybe you're right," said Big John, and he did not look at me directly. "We know he telegraphed to Inishthorav and told them we were coming, and spoiled our chances of getting back our sheep, ay, and maybe landed King Cooney's young son Colm into the height of trouble as well."

I had never thought of this. If he had told all about Colm, it would mean that he cared for no one but himself. I remembered his hard eyes, like a seagull's eyes. And then I remembered his care of all our old people from Mamó down, and of our sick men, women and children, and how he had done every single thing a human being could do to make them comfortable and to cure their ills. He was surely a strange mixture. But even to myself I did not want to admit that he was capable of telling the Guards and the whole world about our caves. There would be a fine revenge for the men of Inishthorav! They could sit back in their godless island then and laugh, knowing that poverty and humiliation would have come together to Inishgillan, and that our people would never again be able to lift up their heads.

While all this flashed through my mind, Big John was saying:

"Let every man be silent when the doctor goes down the slip. Let no one disgrace us all with an uncharitable word, or worse still, with a blow, no matter how black your hearts may be. We kept him against his will. He's within his rights to want to go. We were foolish to think we could be friendly with him. People must always pay for that kind of foolishness."

"'Twas a sorry day for us that we ever saw that doctor!"

Bartley MacDonagh said in a voice of despair.

All over the room the men muttered agreement. I began to move towards the door, hardly lifting my feet, as if a new heaviness had got into them. I noticed that the men made way for me, and it seemed to me as if I were already marked with a little of the distrust that they had in the doctor. I was his apprentice, after all, and his closest friend.

I felt the air of the kitchen heavy with their anger and I wanted to get out and breathe the sweet fresh air of the Atlantic. Worst of all to see was the line of old women sitting on a bench by the fire, all their old heads bent, and their hands busy with their rosary beads under their aprons. This was just how they looked when the men were all out in the currachs and a storm sprang up, or in a wet summer when we could not dry the turf, or when the news came over the telegraph from Galway that prices were bad at the fair. I could not help feeling responsible for all this misfortune, though my wits told me it was not all my fault that we had kept the doctor. Every man in this kitchen was as responsible as I was. Still, since it was I and Roddy who had hidden him on the first day, there was no avoiding the fact that the original idea to keep him had been ours. What pricked my conscience most was the knowledge that if I had the same choice over again, I would make the same decision. I could never regret having learned from the doctor so many things that had been shut off from me before, things that made the whole world a different place for me.

Outside, I found Roddy waiting for me, leaning against the wall of the house.

"I thought you'd never come," he said in a hissing

whisper. "Stephen Conneeley is gone off up the road, looking for Simon, I suppose. And look down there!"

I looked where he pointed, away out to sea, where the Pilot Boat was half-way over from the Aran Islands. It was a calm, pale-blue sea, of the kind that you get only in early summer. Against it the Pilot Boat looked black as soot, and the smoke streaming from her funnel hung black against the pale-blue sky. It was by the amount of smoke that I knew it was the Pilot Boat. Probably Mattie O'Brien was on her, I thought, if he could make an excuse to come and watch the downfall of the Inishgillan men.

"She'll be at the slip in half an hour," I said.

"Any minute now," said Roddy, "someone will come out of Big John's kitchen and see her, and then the men will all march down to the slip to wait for the Guards to land. We had better go to the cave now and bring the doctor to the slip—"

"You must go to the cave alone," I said.

"Is it let the doctor out of that bunk and walk the length of the island with him?" Roddy looked terrified at the prospect. "I'd as soon walk alone with a wild animal. Can't we both go?"

"When the people see the Pilot Boat, they'll all go to the slip," I said. "That will leave the rest of the island deserted except for Simon and Stephen and the two of ourselves."

"And the doctor."

"Yes, and a few old women, that wouldn't have the strength to chase a cat away from the chickens. The two of us alone would never be able to defend him."

"Defend him! God preserve us! Do you think they would attack him with the two of us as witnesses?"

"They might, if they thought that no one would

believe our story. Or they might be so sure that we would never tell the Guards of an Inishgillan man's crime that they would think they could safely make away with him even if we were watching. I'm sure they think that most of the men would be delighted to hear that the doctor was—out of the way."

"Faith, then, they'd be making a mistake," said Roddy hotly. "I'd call the Guards myself for a crime like that. If all the men knew we had the doctor in the cave! I hope we'll never have to tell where we put him."

"Maybe there won't be any need. I'm thinking that you should go to the cave and let the doctor out, and trot him along to the slip as fast as you can. I'll go and search for Simon and Stephen and keep them in talk, or maybe send them in the wrong direction if I can. You can tell the doctor not to talk, that it'll be dangerous, if he starts complaining. But I'm thinking he's past that stage now, the poor man."

I could see that Roddy could not forget what he had suffered from the doctor's tongue in the first weeks that we had him. Still he made no more objections. Without another word, he climbed over the wall and began to cross the little fields that lay between us and the slip, jumping like a hare this way and that as he avoided the humps and hollows in the ground.

I did not wait to see him turn in the direction of the caves. Stephen Conneeley had gone up the hill, Roddy had said. Quickly I climbed up the grassy slope at the other side of the road, walking among the sheep, until I came to a high point from which I could see all the middle of the island. There was Stephen, walking along a by-road a quarter of a mile beyond our house. He was going towards the sea. If I did not cut him off quickly, he might even meet Roddy on his way to the caves.

I sprang down the hill, flung myself over the wall onto the road, and ran as fast as my lungs and my legs would let me. I made no effort to be quiet, nor to conceal my excitement and agitation. I came pounding up behind Stephen, so that he whirled around in fright.

"The doctor!" I panted wildly. "Have you seen the doctor?"

"No, then," Stephen said softly. "Why are you looking for the doctor?"

"They're saying he's going away! They're saying he's going off with the Guards, and we won't have him any more!"

"They're saying that, are they?"

"Yes, and all the wonders he was telling me, I'll hear no more of them. I want to find him, wherever he is, and have a last talk with him, for I'm thinking 'twill be a long time before I have a chance to talk with his like again."

"It might be, then," Stephen said, still very softly. "Will I help you to find him, agrá?"

"Do, please, Stephen! Wait a moment." I began to climb the wall by the side of the road. "If I stand up there on the rocks, I might catch a sight of him."

I jumped down into the field by the road and made for a pile of rocks in the middle of it.

"I'll come with you, agrá," said Stephen.

I could hear him clambering up the rocks behind me, as agile as a goat. A moment after I stood erect on the top, there he was beside me. We gazed all around. There was a fine view from up there. In every direction, the walls of the fields seemed to wriggle like worms, encircling the oddly-shaped fields. The Pilot Boat was much nearer to the slip now, and I could see a trickle of figures on the road that led down there. Already the boat had been observed, of course, and soon the road would be black with people going down to meet it. Slowly I swung around, following with my eyes the direction that Roddy had taken. The path he was on was not visible from up here, as I knew, except when it came near the slip. I turned away from the sea and looked up towards Mamó's house. And there, on another by-road parallel with ours, was Simon.

Stephen saw him at the same moment that I did. He let out a piercing whistle, that made me jump and stagger with the suddenness of it. Simon stopped in his tracks and cocked his head like a dog. Then he saw us and began to wave his arms. Stephen let out several more whistles, two short, one long, three short. This was their way of calling, "Come here!" I had often heard them at it when I was working at gathering weed from the strand below their house.

Immediately Simon turned back to the main road and started to come towards us. As we got down off the rocks and hurried to meet him, Stephen said to me:

"I could be shouting all day and he'd never turn his head. A whistle brings him like a shot."

One would think he was talking about a dog, with the way he said it.

When I found myself standing between the two brothers, suddenly I was frightened. The two identical faces had something to do with it, I suppose, the glaring brown eyes and big solid teeth that gave them a snarling expression. Still Stephen spoke softly as ever when he said:

"Simon, Patcheen is looking for the doctor same as ourselves. Did you get a sight of him at all?"

"Sight nor sound, hair nor hide," said Simon. "I've looked high up and low down, in and out, every place I know. You know where he is!" he said to me suddenly. "You're always with him. You should know where he'd go if he wanted to hide. Where is he?"

"Now, now, not so rough," said Stephen. He turned back to me. "'Tis true, agrá, you're always with him. You should be able to think where he'd go. Where would he go ahide?"

"Why should he hide? Doesn't he live here as free as ourselves?"

"He might hide until the Guards would come, for fear someone would do away with him and tell the Guards there was never such a man here—"

Suddenly I looked from one of them to the other and then I knew what to do. I began to run. Behind me I heard the twins call out:

"Stop! Stop!"

"Come back, agrá!" This was Stephen, of course, but he did not sound very loving in spite of the name he was calling me. Then I heard him whistle, two long, one short, three long, and a moment later they were running after me, as light as two greyhounds.

When I was a small boy, I often had a nightmare about being chased along this very road in the dead of night by a big black pooka, who almost grabbed me by my shirt-tails as I leaped in through my own door. Often in the morning I would go out to see if he had left the prints of his two black paws on either side of the door. My mother used to laugh, and she would say that these things never happen. Yet here I was now with no less than two pookas on my tail, and it was no less terrifying for happening in the broad daylight. Thoughts flashed through my head. I might trip on a stone and fall. I could feel them pounce on me. I might not be able to run fast enough. They would grab me by an arm each and whisk me off the road. None of it would matter so long as Roddy reached the doctor safely and made him run back to the slip. It would take a boy half an hour to run from the cave to the slip. With the doctor it would certainly be slower. Yet here I was already almost at the slip myself. Through a kind of mist I saw the Guards already standing on dry land and Luke's currach that had brought them ashore bobbing up and down beside the slip. There were six Guards and Mattie O'Brien, grinning like a devil, standing a little behind them.

It seemed to me that the whole population of the island was there. They stood in two groups quite silent, with a passageway between them ready for the Guards to walk through. The children were not running around plaguing everybody, as they would have been doing at any other time. Instead they were pressed in against their mothers' skirts, and there was not a word out of any of them.

Every head was turned when I was seen galloping down the hill, followed by the twin Conneeleys. I saw my mother throw up her apron to cover her face, as if this were the final humiliation. I had no time to care for that. I ran straight to Big John, who was in the middle of a courtly speech of welcome to the Sergeant of the Guards.

When they took in the fact that the Guards had already arrived, the twins dropped back a little. I raised my voice so as to make sure that they and all the people would hear, and called out:

"The doctor is on his way. He'll be here in a few minutes."

Big John looked at me, astonished at the interruption. Then he said:

"We can go up to my house, then, and wait—"

"No, no!" In front of all the people and the Guards as well, how could I tell what I feared? "We'll wait here. He's coming here, to the slip. We'll wait here, all together."

"We'll wait here, as the boy says," said the Sergeant, looking at me sharply.

I saw Big John and my father glance at each other and then clamp their mouths tightly shut. I was never so glad of our Inishgillan habit of being silent before strangers. I could not have answered one of their questions in that company.

There we stood and waited. Not another word was said, but somehow all the people came gradually to feel that something strange was happening. Since I had spoken, naturally every face was turned inland, watching for the doctor to come down the road. I had not said from which direction he would come. Now one by one, they began to turn slowly to look out to sea again, and a look of desperation that was terrible to see came over their faces.

A hundred yards out from the slip, two currachs were hove to. Behind them were three or four more, and as we watched, more and more kept coming until there was a little navy of them there. Those of us that had good sight knew what had brought them. It was the men of Inishthorav, come out in force, to watch and enjoy our downfall. There they sat, holding the currachs easily in position with an occasional dip of the oars, grinning and pointing and laughing as if they were at a circus. I heard the old women whisper to each other:

"Who are they? What brought them here?"

Then, as they learned who the men in the currachs were, a soft whining sound began among them, like a dog trying to get into the kitchen on a winter's night. Mamó was among them, and it went through my heart to see her swaying back and forth with grief.

It was while this was going on that Roddy and the doctor appeared on the little path that ran along the top of the strand by the slip. I was mighty glad to see them, because until that moment I had been in doubt as to whether the doctor would have come alive out of his hiding-place. A growl of rage went up from the men. The Sergeant took a step forward. The crowd parted a little more, leaving a wide space for the doctor, as if their hatred forced them back from him.

At the edge of this space the doctor paused and looked down between the ranks of the people, at the Sergeant. In the painful silence, we saw him lift his eyes to the currachs out on the sea, and we saw the light of understanding come into his eyes. He began to move towards the Sergeant, and then an extraordinary thing happened.

Suddenly old Mamó burst out of the group of women that were gathered at one end of the crowd. She rushed across the space that separated them from the doctor, threw herself on her knees by his side and seized his hand. Then, very slowly, she bent her head and kissed his hand, as if he had been a bishop, and we heard her say clearly:

"God bless you always, and reward you for all the good you did on Inishgillan. God speed you and protect you everywhere you go."

The doctor looked down at her, making no attempt to pull his hand away. Indeed it seemed to me that he was holding her hands in his. The Sergeant came a little closer, uncertainly, and said:

"You are the doctor? We came to take you to Galway. You can come with us now, on the Pilot Boat."

Now the moment has come, I thought. Now Big John will be arrested, and my father. Such a thing had never happened on Inishgillan before. Now they would be brought away on the Pilot Boat, and we would hear no more of them except when we would gather in at Luke's place in the evening and hear on the radio of the trial and condemnation of the two desperate criminals from Inishgillan. Already I could imagine how the Galway people would smile at each other and say:

"Don't we all know they're a bit savage out on the islands?"

This thought made my fists clench with fury. I looked around at the men and saw that all of them were almost choking with the yells of rage that they would not give. Big John had said that they were to be silent. Not a word, not a blow, he had said. The Sergeant looked frightened. He flicked his fingers and the Guards moved closer in behind him. The pause seemed to last for an age, before we heard the doctor say calmly:

"Why should I go with you? I'm spending the rest of the summer on Inishgillan, and longer if I like it as well as I have done up to now."

"But you were shipwrecked. The whole world thought you were drowned," the Sergeant stuttered.

"Then perhaps a few prayers were said for me," said the doctor. "They'll do me no harm."

"But you should have been sent into Galway with the captain of the *Coriander*. The Inishgillan men kept you here against your will. We got instructions to take you by force if necessary and convey you into Galway on the Pilot Boat."

"Young man," said the doctor, "there is no law that says a man must report that he was shipwrecked. And if you attempt to convey me by force or otherwise into Galway, I think that my good friends here will see to it that you get something to remember them by."

"Threatening a member of the Civic Guards is an offence against the law," said the poor Sergeant, not knowing how to answer this. He seemed to gasp for words before he succeeded in going on: "In the name of all that's wonderful, why was I brought out here? I have something better to do than to spend the day tossing on the wide ocean. Why was I told you were a prisoner here, when a child could see that you're surrounded with friends? And you don't look a bit like a prisoner—you look to me as strong as a Protestant. Was it out to fool me they were?"

And he turned to glare out at the Inishthorav men in their currachs, still sitting waiting, I suppose, for the chains to be put on some of the Inishgillan men.

"'Twas a little bit of jealousy, I suppose," said Big John smoothly, "having no doctor themselves, maybe. Now 'tis best for you to do as I asked you a while ago, and that's to come up to my place for a drop of the hard stuff and a little bite to eat, maybe, and you can be telling us all the doings in Galway while you're at it."

And this was what was done. Out on the sea, the Inishthorav men were jumping like a school of porpoises when they saw us all walk up the road together, Guards and doctor and all, singing and laughing as if we were at a wedding. Old Mamó's arm was linked in the doctor's and she hardly took her eyes off him as long as the

Guards remained on the island. They had insisted that
Mattie come with them too, though he had wanted to
wait for them on the Pilot Boat. Through the rest of the
day he sat silently glaring, eating and drinking everything
he was offered and never saying a word.

The Sergeant and the Guards enjoyed the hospitality
of the island until it was time for them to start back for
Galway. By that time they were so cheerful that they
never noticed that no one invited them to come again.
As Big John said:

"They're nice, friendly kind of people. 'Tis a pity we
can't ask them to come back. But glory be to God! No one
on Inishgillan would ever again close an eye if he
thought the Guards might drop in any day without
warning, for a chat."

Things were different on Inishgillan after that. The
doctor stayed with us for more than a year. When the
winter came on, and the black, stormy evenings, with
the darkness rushing over the ocean at five o'clock in the
afternoon, we thought he would get tired of us and be
gone. But he had something to do, he said, and he would
not rest until he had done it. This was to make peace
between the Inishgillan men and the men of Inishthorav.
He wanted this mostly for Manus Griffin's sake.

As Manus got older, he wished more and more to see
his daughter Peggy again, and his fine grandchildren
that were living on Inishthorav. He often spoke to the
doctor of his longing to have one of Peggy's sons to
succeed him as the weaver on Inishgillan.

"'Twas my great-great-grandfather that built this
loom," he said, "and it will feel it if the hand that works
it when I'm gone hasn't got a drop of my blood in it."

Almost at once, the doctor sent word to Inishthorav

that he would go to them if one of them was sick and needed his help. The first time they sent for him, Big John offered to send a bodyguard with him. But he would have no one but myself only. On Inishthorav, we were treated with civility. The people were afraid of us, and yet they needed our services. I looked about for Colm Cooney, but he kept out of sight that first evening.

The patient was a young man that had had his foot broken by a falling stone when he was building a house. We fixed him up with everything he needed. It gratified me to see the Inishthorav men admiring my skill with bandages, and I saw how impressed they were when the doctor left it to me to give instructions about what the patient should eat and how he should be cared for until we came again.

On the way back to Inishgillan, the doctor sat facing me in the currach. When we were well out from the shore he said:

"You would make a good doctor, Pat."

"Never," I said. "Do you think I would ever have the courage to take the knife in my hand and open up a man's body, and cut away a part of him, and stitch him up again? Never in this life!"

"If you were to try that now you would do murder," said the doctor calmly, "but if you were to go to the university in Galway, you would learn how to do that and a lot of other things that I can never teach you here."

"I'll never get to learn them then," I said, "because I could never go to the university. That costs money, and besides I'm too ignorant."

"You could learn. And money is not as scarce as you think."

Several times when we were making our rounds he

said the same things, until at last I said in despair:

"How do I know that I would be able to learn those things? If I leave the island and go to Galway for seven long years, maybe at the end of it I'll be as backward as I am now. How do you know that I would ever make a doctor?"

"You can trust me."

"How do you know?"

"I know because when my life was in danger you let me hide in your caves, that no one but an Inishgillan man had ever seen before. You put my life before everything else. And you said you would rather die ten times than have me lose my life. Those things prove that you would make a doctor for Inishgillan and for the other islands too. But perhaps in Galway you would forget about the islands, and go off to another part of Ireland where you would get money, like big John's nephew in Boston."

"I would never forget about the islands. I would come back for certain sure."

It was then that he told me how it was that he could care so well for our sick people, at the same time as planning to ruin us all by sending for the Guards.

"Every doctor takes an oath that he will do his utmost for the sick, even if they happen to be his mortal enemies. I thought that a man could divide himself in two. I know now that can't be done. It's a funny thing that when the rescue party came, I had no inclination whatever to go with them. It was Mamó that settled it, in the end."

He and Mamó had great consultations during those first weeks. At last it was she who went with him as an ambassador to discuss the future of the Grazing Island.

It was her first visit to Inishthorav for more than thirty years, and she enjoyed it immensely. She found several of her old friends alive, that had not been allowed to speak to her since the sad day of Peggy's wedding. She also searched out Colm Cooney and arranged for him to come and spend some time with her on Inishgillan. That was the real beginning of our life-time friendship with him.

Mamó and the doctor made a treaty with the men of Inishthorav, giving them grazing rights during certain months of the year, and they got them to agree to give back our sheep at once. In return, we gave them presents of some of the things we had got off the *Coriander*.

"'Tis a pity we gave away the lovely suits," said Sidecar. "'Twould be a fine thing to have a navy-blue suit for every man on Inishgillan and on Inishthorav as well."

But all the men agreed that we had got so much from the *Coriander's* wreck that we would never complain about the suits. When I came home from Galway for Christmas, after my first term at the university, I found that someone had made a ballad about the *Coriander*, and all the good things that had come to us because of her: Manus Griffin's daughter Peggy and her six fine sons, all our lost sheep, friendship with the Inishthorav people, and myself gone off to Galway to be a doctor! During the next years, whenever I was inclined to be lazy or idle, I would always hear in my imagination Máirtín Thornton from Béal Mór rolling out the last verse of the ballad that said how I surprised everyone in Galway with my knowledge. You may be sure that this kept me at my work.

Also by Eilís Dillon in Children's Poolbeg

The Singing Cave

The Seekers

The Lion Cub